A HERITAGE OF THE HEART

Georgia Kohart

FLYING SQUIRREL PRESS

ISBN 0-9706348-0-3

A HERITAGE OF THE HEART

formerly published as Cincinnati Belle

by Georgia Kohart

Cover Art – *"A Miami and Erie Packet"* –
Courtesy of Toledo/Lucas County Library

Cover Design – Hope Wallace Cartwright

Photography – Royal Images

Printed in the U.S.A.

DEDICATION

I thank my husband, Tim, who is my loving editor, creative consultant and cheerleader, for his enthusiastic and unwavering support and for believing in me. Thank you to Wendy Bryant for her editing assistance. Thanks to Linda and Gary Hodges for use of the "Old Brick" and to Ann Miller for sharing her knowledge of family history. I owe a great debt to my late mother and father-in-law, Gladys and T. Frank Kohart for opening up the fascinating world of Paulding County history. I'm grateful to my parents, Clyde O. and the late Clara Wallace, for instilling respect for Ohio and United States history.

To my sister Hope and kindred creative spirit, thanks for listening.

To my daughters, Elizabeth, Ellen and Eve, I say, I love you and use your talents to the fullest.

CHAPTER 1

She tried to convince herself it was all a dream and everything that happened was just the product of a restless night. She could have believed that too, if it hadn't been for the old scrap of linen. Tattered and stained, with its uneven stitching and childish embroidery, she kept it hidden between the pages of a book.

*****

It was hot, too hot even for September. Elizabeth Hudson leaned forward to allow a little air to circulate and cool her sweat-soaked back. The air conditioning in the old Jeep had surrendered long before and there was a rusted out spot under the accelerator that showed glimpses of the asphalt passing underneath. One of these days, she promised herself, she was going to buy a new car. She just wasn't ready to part with the old wreck yet. Too many memories were in it. At any rate, she was almost there.

The young woman's heart gave an extra little bump of excitement as the Jeep neared the familiar turn. Gravel popped and crunched under the tires as she swung the ancient vehicle into the lane, out of the brilliant sunshine and into the cool shade of the huge maples that overhung the drive. Even though she had grown up in a farmhouse about a mile up the road, she had always felt a stronger spiritual connection to the place in front of her.

The old brick federal never changed. Built more than one hundred and sixty years ago, the house had always been in the family. It leaned a little, but then it had always leaned a little. At some point, long rods, called building washers, had been installed in three places to stabilize the structure. These were anchored with big iron stars.

Although she had pulled up to the back of the house, it was

the entry most people used. Beyond was the vegetable garden, the barn and outbuildings, then the tilled fields that stretched off to the woods, then the river, about a half-mile distant. Cicadas rattled unseen from the trees, while other insects of late summer buzzed and clicked in an unwavering rhythm from the dry grasses. The day's sweltering heat shimmered over all. Although there wasn't much sign of life, the dry lawn was maintained and the gardens appeared well tended.

She felt herself relaxing already and took a moment to lean her head of unruly, auburn hair against the headrest and breathe deeply. Her lightly freckled nose wrinkled as she sniffed hungrily at the familiar tangy aroma of tomatoes, vinegar and spices that drifted through the screen door. Gran was making ketchup. The young woman dragged her things out of the Jeep, clumped up the worn, uneven steps and plopped her bags down on the back porch. Her paternal grandmother, Lydia Hudson, appeared behind the screen, wiping her hands on a dishtowel. She must have heard the ancient vehicle rattling and squeaking up the long drive.

On the surface Gran looked pretty much the same as she had at Christmas. Her silvery white hair was arranged in a short, youthful style, and a crisp gingham blouse and jeans belied her years. Lydia prided on taking good care of herself and preserving her youthful appearance with sensible diet, exercise and plenty of activities on the farm and in the county. Her brown eyes still snapped with spirit and vitality.

"Lizzy!"

Gran flung the door open and hugged Elizabeth heartily. The younger woman wrapped her arms around her grandmother. Even though Elizabeth towered over her by a good five inches, she was pulled off balance by the fierce embrace. Lydia had always been slight, but now it felt as if she were a sparrow in Elizabeth's arms. Even so, the elderly woman still had her strength.

Much to Elizabeth's surprise, she felt the warm wetness of Lydia's tears soaking into the shoulder of her shirt. Her grandmother was an emotional rock and had never been the weepy sort. Arms around each other, they squeezed through the door into the dim coolness of the kitchen.

There was a steady click, click, click across the age-worn floorboards and something cold and moist pressed into the back of Elizabeth's leg.

"Forsooth!" She squatted to make over the her grandmother's old Basset Hound, thankful for the chance to break eye contact with her too perceptive grandparent. The old dog's entire back end wriggled ecstatically as his long tail, tipped with a little white spot on the end, lashed back and forth.

Gran stepped back and fumbled in a pocket for a Kleenex. "Looks like Forsooth is glad you're here, too! It's just been way too long!"

Wiping tears from her own cheeks, Elizabeth stood up. The delighted hound continued to gaze adoringly up at her, his capacious tongue lolling as he panted happily.

"I just wanted to spend some time with you, relax a little and help you out with the garden like I used to do. And while I'm here, I need to do a little more research at the library and the county historical society for my thesis."

What she didn't say was that she had been busy with working and classes for the past three years because she wanted it that way. She purposefully tried not to let herself have too much time to think…or feel.

Elizabeth was glad she had decided to use some of her vacation time to come to her Grandmother's farm for a visit. Even though Gran had managed well and run the farm on her own for more than twenty years, time was taking its toll.

"I want to hear all the exciting things you've been doing! You must be relieved to be finishing school. And Heaven knows I could use some help in the garden. It would be a shame for all that bounty to rot on the vine for want of picking. I don't know why I planted so much. I won't ever eat it all, even with the help of your parents. Just habit, I guess." She sighed and shrugged her shoulders.

"I've spent about every waking minute that I'm not in the O.R. either in class, cooped up in my apartment hunched over the computer, or wading through the stacks at the University's medical library. It's real exciting," she said dryly.

"That's what I would have guessed by looking at you. You look like you never see the light of day." Gran replied. Never one to mince words, she eyed her granddaughter, her only son's youngest, closely. "Are you *really* all right?"

Forsooth pawed Elizabeth's leg and to avoid the question that hung unanswered in the air, she quickly knelt back down to the dog to lavish him with more attention. With great speed and expertise, he planted a slobbery kiss right on her mouth.

"He never misses does he?" Elizabeth sputtered. Quickly standing, she scrubbed at her wet face with her shirttail.

Gran leaned back against the kitchen counter, arms folded, and shook her head, laughing.

"Nope, Lizzie, never!"

It was good to be home.

CHAPTER 2

The next morning, a Saturday, Elizabeth woke before Gran, who was the original early bird. Still clad in the T-shirt and boxers in which she'd slept, she padded quietly around the kitchen, preparing a pot of coffee and toasting a bagel. Balancing a plate and a piping hot mug of coffee, she made her way to the porch and settled into her favorite rocker to enjoy the day's beginning.

As she was slipping out the screen door, she felt a familiar cold, damp pressure on her leg. She looked down and smiled at Forsooth.

"Call me anything, just don't call me late for supper, right, boy?" She went back to the kitchen and slipped a couple of dog treats out of the box in the cupboard. "Always receptive to a snack, aren't you? Well, so am I."

The dog shuffled along and established himself comfortably within range of potential crumbs.

Sipping the steaming coffee, Elizabeth gazed out over the yard, through the few remaining trees in the orchard and past the meadow to the abandoned canal, from which trailed a few veils of morning fog. The sun was just clearing the distant fields on its upward trek. Even that early in the morning it was obvious it was going to be another sweltering day. Humidity already hung heavy over the farm.

Mitch would have loved this, she thought, even though he was a city kid right down to his socks. After his first trip out here, he was hooked on country life, not to mention Gran's cooking. She sighed, thinking about the times they had watched the sun come up from this very spot, just the two of them.

Except for the sounds of the wild creatures and the weather, the farm she remembered from her youth was silent now. The chicken house, once full of busy hens and the strident crow of mean Jack the rooster, was quiet. Livestock no longer occupied the red hip-roofed barn and sheds. Her father and oldest brother farmed the tillable acreage, so the buildings only housed equipment. Although the activity of earlier years had ceased, the stillness created a sense of serenity, rather than decay.

The fields only changed as the crops rotated - wheat, corn, and then soy beans. Nor did the woods, except for an occasional tree felled by age or the elements.

A cardinal called "what-cheer, what-cheer" from a nearby spruce tree and a single cricket chirped sleepily under the porch. A wren, pert tail flashing, chattered from the tip of a picket on the fence around Gran's herb garden, defending his nest in a little red birdhouse that hung nearby. Cautiously a wild rabbit loped through the ancient orchard. It stopped to nibble nervously on a fallen apple. The only response from Forsooth, sprawled at Elizabeth's feet, was the twitch of a paw. The rabbit continued its meal unmolested. The gnarled trunks and twisted branches of the fruit trees brought to mind a story her grandfather told about the old orchard.

Pap, who had been the one to start calling her "Lizzie," had died when she was in junior high school. Always one to relish a good story, he used to relate how Johnny Appleseed had planted the original orchard at the "Old Brick," as everyone referred to the house. Those infamous trees were gone long before he was born.

After harvest, when he had more time, Elizabeth and Pap used to spend hours in the woods, fields and barns. Elizabeth's two older brothers, when they weren't helping Dad with the tractors and equipment, playing football or basketball, were more interested in tinkering with their dilapidated cars so they could take dates to the movies at the county seat on Saturday nights. That left just her and Pap.

"Lizzie," he grunted as he brought a palm-sized rock down on the hard, tan shell of a hickory nut, "you know you can do anything you want with your life. "Go off and go to college, like you want. Your brothers are. We all expect you to. But, don't ever forget where you come from."

It was late November of the year she was thirteen. She and

Pap were sitting in the warm, dry basement of the brick house and cracking some of the nuts they'd gathered earlier in the fall. Scuffing through the October leaves, they'd gone to the big trees in the woods and filled a feed sack to bulging with black walnuts and hickory nuts, leaving plenty behind for the squirrels and other wild folk. It was to be the last time they would roam the woods together because Pap would die suddenly of a heart attack before Christmas.

"Oh, Pap," she'd said, giggling and popping a nut meat into her mouth, "I know where I come from."

"Oh, well, I didn't mean that," he chuckled. "Lizzie, someday you'll understand." He whacked another hickory and handed it to Elizabeth, who had the task of picking the nuts out of their shells.

"My ancestors, and yours too, were some of the first white people to settle in this area. The land was payment for military service during the War of 1812. Ohio was at the western edge of the United States then, a wilderness. I'm not proud of the fact that they're coming meant that the natives who were already here had to leave But, I do take pride in knowing that I come from stock that was tough enough to stick it out. Life wasn't easy back then, you know."

He paused and selected another handful of nuts. "We've been farmers all down the line, since the time that crops were planted around the huge stumps left behind after the big timber was cut down. But we weren't the first ones."

Taking another sip of coffee, Elizabeth thought about her grandfather's impressive library filled predominantly with books pertaining to politics, American and Ohio history and geography. In the county, he had been regarded as an authoritative source of local history.

"I've been a farmer all my life, just like my dad. I'm not proud of the fact that I didn't finish high school, but there was a depression on and I was needed here." "That didn't keep me from reading everything I could get my hands on, though."

He took great delight in sharing the things he learned.

Elizabeth had heard her grandfather's stories before, but never tired of them. Pap's tales were animated with mystery, daring and intrigue, causing her to wish she'd been born into a more exciting time.

Some of the best times with him were the hours spent crouched over the furrows in the fields closest to the river, searching for flint arrowheads and prehistoric tools. He would hold up an artifact and announce "scraper" or "pestle," then stand and give her the treasure to add to her collection.

"Boy," he'd say, while wiping his face with the ever present bandana from the back pocket of his striped overalls, "I'd give just about anything to go back about 500 years and stand here and see it all exactly like it was."

He launched into the history of the land and the people who occupied it thousands of years before white men even knew it existed. The rich earth along the Auglaize River had been tilled by ancient peoples for almost more years than anyone could count. They tended their fields of squash, corn and beans near villages along the life-giving stream.

"By 1822, they were gone," Pap said, shaking his head, "much to our shame. The Ottawa's were removed by the American government to a reservation in Kansas."

He'd loved every inch of the land he worked and never took for granted the value of a simple life of hard work. In his mind, and he had been right, there was no higher calling than an honest occupation that served other people, and for him that was growing crops and raising livestock. As they cracked the black walnuts and hickory nuts destined for Gran's big blue mixing bowl to be used for Thanksgiving recipes, he had tried to share that knowledge with her.

When people heard she was originally from northwestern Ohio, it seemed they felt compelled to remark on the lack of scenery and any other items of interest in state's upper corner. True, the area was flat, but it held a subtle beauty. It was in the lush green oceans of corn and soybeans. In July, the ripe wheat shone in a golden swath under the hot sun.

The pioneers that had traveled to the newly opened lands after the Indian Wars, found endless forests of oak, hickory, beech and buckeye, all part of the Great Black Swamp. They continued farming the fields left behind by the Ottawa tribe and started clearing the big trees, leaving massive stumps to be yanked or burned out of the ground.

Elizabeth agreed with her grandfather, that her forebears must have been cut from pretty tough cloth. She, too, was capable. She was employed as a circulating nurse in thoracic surgery at University Hospital and was working toward her master's degree in nursing. Her job took stamina, but she suspected she would have wilted into a useless, whining lump after a day of hauling wood, slopping hogs and cooking over an open fire, not to mention bearing and raising a passel of stair-step kids.

Unbidden, her thoughts drifted to the hardest task she had ever faced.

CHAPTER 3

Personally, Elizabeth felt that the cruelest work was losing, to death, the person she loved more than anything in the world. She had watched her husband disappear before her eyes. Cancer had consumed his life, devouring him day by day, and toward the end, hour by hour.

One day, near the end, when she thought he was asleep, she had, for long minutes, stared at him. She'd willed her eyes to photograph his image and burn an imprint in her brain. Her eyes really did begin burn. But the heat was only from unshed tears. Suddenly Mitch woke.

"What are you doing," he asked softly, reaching out to her.

"Trying to memorize you," she admitted, because they didn't have many secrets. Her tears blazed tracks down her face and onto his hand.

All her medical training and expertise couldn't keep Mitch from slipping away. Her memorization didn't work, either. Unless she had a photo, it was getting more and more difficult to recall his face. She didn't want him to fade away, but she knew couldn't mourn forever. She hadn't been able to alleviate Mitch's pain, and for the past three years, she hadn't been very successful at easing her own.

Elizabeth knew that was why she had come back. She had returned not only to visit her beloved Gran, but also to wander along the fencerows, walk through the trees, sit in the haymow and explore Pap's world once again. Even though he was gone, she knew she would still feel his comforting presence. She would need it, because she knew it was time to think and feel again. She wanted to know more than work and study. Back in these peaceful surroundings, Elizabeth hoped to begin to accept Mitch's death. She wanted to commence the journey back to living, but hadn't quite been able to take the first step out of her grief.

Even though she wasn't in the O.R., doing research, or sitting in class, she couldn't let down. Not yet. She wanted to do it right, completely and in an orderly manner. Once again she pushed back the surge of pain and swiped the tears from her eyes with the back of her arm. For now, Elizabeth had to maintain control just as she had for the past three years.

She had a few things to do first. Mom and Dad were expecting her for lunch. She wanted to hear what activities they had planned for the family while she was home. There would be a big cookout that would include her brothers Tom and Nathan, their wives and kids, Gran, some aunts and uncles, a few of the closest neighbors and a couple of Elizabeth's old friends from high school. Mom would want to make at least one all-day shopping trip, hit a couple malls and enjoy a nice lunch. Elizabeth's lips curved in a weak smile as she recognized her mother's old tactics from her childhood: *When life gives you lemons, go shopping.* Staying very busy was still her mode of operation. It usually worked. Perhaps that was why Elizabeth was prone to the same mindset.

For the moment though, she was determined to enjoy the sunrise and her coffee. She propped her bare feet up on the porch rail, took another sip of coffee and continued musing about the old canal that she could see running parallel to Gran's farm.

The old Miami and Erie Canal was just across the road from the Old Brick and ran on past the farm where Elizabeth had grown up, about a mile down the road. About a half-mile north of her childhood home, the Wabash and Erie Canal joined the Miami and Erie at a right angle. The Wabash began there and headed west, toward Fort Wayne, Indiana. At that intersection there was once a town, simply called, Junction. Originally platted in 1842, the little village had bustled with homes, several churches, many thriving businesses and plenty of saloons.

Once again, Elizabeth could hear Pap's voice as he recounted the rollicking canal days. He usually shared canal stories when they sat on one of many tumbled stone blocks, relics of the old waterway, and fished.

"Until the railroads pushed through this part of the country and forced them into obsolescence, these man-made canals functioned as water highways. For the first time since carving an existence out of the Great Black Swamp, there was a way for farmers to ship goods back east and make a decent profit of it," he said, lifting his line out of the water to check the bait.

"Dang! Nibbled it right off while I was flappin' my jaws. Serves me right for being so longwinded," he muttered while digging around in the battered coffee can full of nightcrawlers.

He flicked the fishing pole and the freshly baited hook dropped neatly into the water with a little "ploop." Settling back, he continued his tale.

"No longer did the fruits of the harvest rot for lack of safe, affordable and reliable transportation."

"Oh, Pap, you sound just like our social studies book," Elizabeth teased. "But, somehow, I like it better hearing it from you."

He picked another worm out of the can and pretended to drop it on her head.

"That'll teach you to be so sassy, youngun'!" He said. "I bet that textbook of yours doesn't say anything about the fact that once upon a time, Junction was expected to pass Fort Wayne and Toledo right by."

He had gone on to tell her about the brief, spanning only a few decades, hey-day of the manmade waterways. The advent of railroads proved to be the undoing for the engineering feat. Although some towns survived and thrived, Junction and dozens of other little settlements along the canals became ghost towns, or at best, tiny crossroads of house trailers, trash and junked cars. Most of the complicated system of aqueducts, locks and bridges servicing the Ohio canals were gone now. The shallow feeder lakes had evolved into recreation areas. A few state parks were developed around restored sections, but most miles of the canals were relegated to the lowly role of roadside ditches or were bulldozed. Few signs of the era remained.

Thinking about how enamored she'd been of her grandfather's historic tales, she half wondered why she hadn't majored in history instead of nursing. She liked a little more action, she decided.

Forsooth, awake now, was snuffling around the weathered boards of the porch floor for bagel crumbs. Catching the tantalizing scent of rabbit from the orchard, he bellowed loud enough to wake Gran, sleeping in her upstairs bedroom at the front of the house. The basset bounded out over the steps in a single leap and tore across the yard in determined pursuit. The rabbit sprinted over the road into the sheltering underbrush along the old canal. Forsooth did not give up and disappeared into a tangle of ironweed, goldenrod and wild asters that fringed the roadside.

Gran had attempted to train Forsooth to stay off the road. Although he was usually compliant, the lure of a scurrying critter was irresistible.

"Forsooth!" Elizabeth cajoled. "C'mere, boy!"

She tried whistling between her fingers like her brothers had taught her, but Forsooth was not interested.

"Aw, c'mon, get back here!"

The only response was a rustle and the snapping of weed stalks. The sound quickly faded, indicating that the distance between the dog and the farm was increasing rapidly. The last thing Gran needed was to have her constant companion hit by a car.

"Don't make me have to come after you," Elizabeth said feebly, even as she was getting out of her comfortable seat.

Spotting a pair of Gran's garden clogs lying by the back door, she quickly crammed her feet into them and limped after the errant dog in the too-small shoes.

"Stupid dog!" She muttered, awkwardly crossing the yard, its grass still wet with dew. The fact that the tranquility of her morning was shattered thoroughly irritated her.

Once across the road, the fuming rescuer fought her way through waist high weeds. With blackberry brambles clawing at her bare calves, she scrambled up the embankment of the canal, hoping the slight elevation would provide a better advantage. Perhaps it would enable her to locate the delinquent dog.

She stood on the old towpath of the canal. Here teams of horses had once plodded steadily, pulling the long, low canal boats, laden with goods, people or both. This section of the canal still contained water. Not much more than a shallow creek lined with cattails, it was dark and murky as an old bottle. Only the plop of a frog disturbed the green surface. Forsooth was nowhere to be seen or heard. Elizabeth headed down the path in the direction he had run, toward a grove of willows with branches trailing, curtain-like, to the ground.

There was not a breath of air. Dusty leaves hung tired and motionless from the trees. Even at that early hour the sun beat down with intensity. She mopped the sweat from her face with her T-shirt. Suddenly the perspiration on her skin chilled as if touched by a breeze. Cool, dank air, like that issuing from a damp basement on a hot day, flowed over her body. Stopping in mid-step, Elizabeth carefully looked around. Everything remained calm, the sun continued to blaze; the surrounding trees remained calm, unruffled by any wind. The hair on the back of her neck stirred and she shivered as she resumed walking.

All was quiet and still, except for the clatter of insects in the tall grasses and birdsong from the trees. The sun beat down on the cracked earth of the towpath. A few steps ahead were the remnants of a decimated canal lock. Over a hundred years before it had raised and lowered the level of the water, enabling the canal boats to safely and easily change elevation. Now the rectangular slabs of stone were scattered about like moss-covered toy blocks. Clambering over them, she continued her search for Forsooth. Elizabeth had spent many hours exploring the canal without fear when she was a child. But for some reason, on this day, she felt uneasy.

As she drew closer to the weeping willows that draped over the walkway, a terrific gust of frigid air practically lifted her off her feet. It pushed the damp, auburn strands of hair from her forehead and flattened her clothing to her body, causing her shirt-sleeves and shorts to flutter in the bitter wind.

Squinting against the tempest, Elizabeth tried to move forward. A clammy mist collected and swirled around her feet, in spite of the gale. It swirled upward, first wrapping her legs, then her torso in a spiral of gauzy haze.

Then on that strange current came noises echoing from a great distance. She heard the murmur of voices punctuated by muted laughter, the hollow swash of water, and a rhythmic thumping accompanied by creaking and metallic jingling. Above it all she heard a mournful call, a horn of sorts, blasting three short notes, then a man's tenor voice sang out in a minor key, a half song, half chant, up and down the scale with each syllable: "hey-ay-a-a-ay…"

"Lizzie!"

Elizabeth whirled around. The wind immediately ceased to whistle past her ears and all was still once again, except for Gran, who was standing in her bathrobe on the back porch of the Old Brick with hands cupped around her mouth.

"Elizabeth! What in heaven's name are you doing up there? And in your pj's, too!"

Shakily, Elizabeth shouted back: "I - I'm looking for… for…*Forsooth*?"

There he was, lying comfortably at Lydia's feet on the top step of the porch, panting happily.

CHAPTER 4

Elizabeth spent the rest of the morning catching up on her laundry while Gran brought her up to date on the local gossip. After lunch with her parents, she returned to the Old Brick to finish unpacking. Hauling her trusty computer and the accompanying equipment up the steep, narrow steps to her room proved to be a hot, sweaty chore. Most of the afternoon was consumed setting up the system. It was aggravating, but she would need it to catalogue her research findings.

She sat cross-legged on a bumpy rag rug surrounded by computer cords and cables. Her reading glasses were perched uselessly on her head, while her nose was buried in the instruction manual. She occasionally recited out loud from the booklet, in hopes that hearing the words, rather than just reading them, would improve her comprehension.

One time, overhearing Elizabeth's sporadic mumbling, Gran stepped to the bottom of the stairs and inquired "Lizzie? You all right?"

Elizabeth grinned, threw her head back and called back: "Yes, Granny, I'm fine, just communing with my computer."

That evening, the two enjoyed a delicious herbed tomato tart. Lydia liked to try new recipes on Elizabeth. After the dishes were done, grandmother and granddaughter relaxed on the porch until the mosquito population forced them to give up and retreat indoors.

It was still quite stuffy inside. The old bricks absorbed and held the heat of the day. Often it was the early morning hours before the house would once again be comfortable. Fortunately a breeze kicked up and promised to blow away some of the humidity and cool the red brick house.

Gran and Elizabeth settled in the living room to watch the late news, then retired. Elizabeth lay in the iron bed with the chipped white paint. It was in her favorite bedroom. The faded pink roses on the wallpaper reminded her of an old hatbox. Forsooth blessed her with his presence. He sprawled across the foot of the bed, snoring lightly. The moon was almost full and shone through the lace curtains at the window, casting fanciful shadows across the wide, uneven floorboards. In the downstairs hall the big Regulator clock bonged the half-hour. "Katy-*did*! Katy-*didn't*!" The ageless insect argument rasped from the woods.

Due to the heat, Elizabeth lay on top of the thin quilt, hands clasped behind her head, staring sightlessly at a crack in the ceiling. A book lay open and face down on her stomach, unread. Although she was physically beat, her mind refused to rest. Leaves stirred in the locust tree outside the window.

Being busy all day had served her well by tiring her body and keeping her from thinking about the strange incident that occurred at sunrise on the old canal towpath. Now, in the stillness of night, there was nothing else to occupy her mind and she was determined to make sense of it. She heaved a sigh. If only Mitch were there with her. He loved a mystery and would have sat up half the night expounding on this theory or that.

Maybe it had just been a dream; perhaps she had dozed off while leaning back in the porch rocker. Or the entire episode could have been one of those deja'vu things. Somewhere in her reading she had run across an article about it. It reported that the feeling of having experienced something before was caused by an electrical short in the synapse between the neurons in the brain. It had felt so real, though.

She took off her glasses, put them and the book on the nightstand and rubbed the bridge of her nose. It was finally cooling down. She plumped her pillow, shoved Forsooth's sleeping carcass over with her feet and slipped between the smooth sheets. Soon she began to relax, gravity won and her eyelids began to droop.

Suddenly, they popped open. She knew one reason why the events of the morning kept nagging! Some of the noises had sounded familiar; she just couldn't place them at the time. The creaking and the metallic jingling, the plodding sound; she recognized them from when she was a kid at 4-H camp. They were sounds made by a horse walking in harness. However, from the top of the towpath, she could see the surrounding countryside for a couple of miles. There hadn't been any horses around. As for the eerie voices and the other things she'd heard, she was no closer to an explanation.

CHAPTER 5

Bright morning light spilled across the old iron bed. Forsooth had abandoned his post earlier to follow the fragrance of waffles down to the kitchen. The combination of sunshine and the aroma of breakfast cooking woke Elizabeth. She stretched, sniffing the delicious air and smiled. She'd slept well, dreamlessly. It felt like she was a kid again, spending the night at Pap and Gran's. Besides, somehow, this bed never felt as empty to her as the one back at her apartment.

Quickly running a brush through her short, russet curls, she slipped on a light cotton robe, scuffed into her slippers and headed down to the kitchen and Gran's pecan waffles.

Elizabeth poured a healthy dollop of syrup on her waffles and made a silent promise that she was not going to worry about calories until she went back. "So, what needs doing most?"

"Oh, let me see." Gran slid her ever-present planner out of her apron pocket. "I would say pick the tomatoes and peppers first. I want to cut them up and freeze them plain. Going to try drying some tomatoes, too. If Martha Stewart can handle it, then so can I! Even bought myself a food dehydrator." She nodded with determination.

"You go, girl!" Elizabeth smiled into her coffee. "Give me a few minutes to dress. I'll shower after the garden work."

"Hey." She paused and attempted to sound nonchalant. "Anybody around get horses recently, I mean since the last time I was home?"

Gran was perusing her little notebook. "Uh, no, not that I know of. Why," she asked, looking up. "Do you want to go riding?"

"No, no. I haven't been on horseback for years! I didn't take a break in order to break a limb! Nope, just thought I heard some horses going by yesterday, that's all…never saw any, though," Elizabeth finished lamely.

Gran was busy scribbling. "No one has horses that I know. Ask your dad, he'd know."

He'd tell me to ask you, that you know more about what goes on around here than he does. More than anybody does. More than is humanly possible." Elizabeth grinned impishly at her Grandmother. "He'd tell me to tell you that."

"Oh, he's a real hoot, that one. A regular comedian. I believe he missed his calling," Gran replied dryly, peering over the top of her glasses. "Say!" she brightened. "Believe it or not, a big biddy hen has been hiding out in the barn. I think she might have gone broody and is sitting on a nest. She's been hanging around for a couple of weeks now, she and a rooster just showed up one day. I wouldn't mind letting them stay, if Forsooth would hear of it, but he chases that rooster off every chance he gets. I miss having chickens." She snapped the notebook shut. "At any rate, I figured maybe while you're scouting around, you might see if you can find her and put out some more food and water."

"You knew I'd be out there, visiting all the old spots, didn't you?"

"Isn't that why you're here?"

Elizabeth got up and gave her grandmother a squeeze. "Gran, I think Dad is right. You *do* know more than is humanly possible."

*****

After a break for a quick salad at lunch, Elizabeth carted the bushel baskets of tomatoes, peppers, zucchini and yellow crook-neck squash she had picked into the kitchen. Then she helped Gran peel, chop and blanch more vegetables than one person could consume in ten winters.

Finally, in exasperation, Elizabeth laid her paring knife down on the counter and turned to her grandmother. "*Lydia*! What in the world are you going to *do* with all this? Mom and Dad have their own garden, too, you know!"

Undeterred by Elizabeth's tone, Gran kept right on chopping. "Well, I'll fill the freezer, of course. I want to can some juice and spaghetti sauce. Your brothers and their broods can put it away when they come to supper, so I like to keep plenty on hand. Let's see, I'll take some to the soup kitchen next time I go into town and Mrs. Buchanan, down the road a piece, well, she's getting up there and can't get around too well anymore. I'll take some to her…"

"Poor ol' Mrs. Buchanan who was pushing a wheelbarrow loaded with stuff from her own garden when I drove past her place the other day?"

"Well, she does overdo," Gran said. "She'll be eighty-one in December."

"Oh, so she's a whoppin' five years older than you?"

"Some people age better than others, you know!" Gran sniffed defensively.

"OK, OK, don't get your knickers in a twist!" Elizabeth laughed, but decided to change the subject.

"I have to go and look up old vital statistics for my thesis tomorrow. Why don't we go out for breakfast - *my* treat!" Elizabeth headed off her grandmother before she had a chance to offer to pay the tab. "Then we can go together to the courthouse and the historical society. Who knows, maybe we'll turn up some dirt on somebody!"

"Elizabeth! I am appalled!" Gran said with mock indignation. "Just what does your thesis pertain to anyway?"

"I don't have an exact title yet, but I'm checking available information on natural deaths in the county. I'm tracking those deaths due to heart disease in rural areas over the past one hundred years and comparing them to present day statistics." Elizabeth grinned at her grandmother. "It should be fun." She laughed at her grandmother's raised eyebrows. "I meant the going out to breakfast part!"

"The county historical society just contacted me about one of your grandfather's ancestors. "She would have been your um…fourth, no, fifth, or might even be sixth great-grandmother. They wondered if I had any information about her. I don't know a lot about the family genealogy when it comes to names and dates. This woman was considered quite talented as an artist. Some of her works are at the historical society. I could go with you to the courthouse and scrounge around and see if I can find any documents and to the county library for old newspapers and such."

By late afternoon a steamy, hot shower felt wonderful on Elizabeth's aching back, despite the fact that the temperature outside hovered at the ninety mark on the rusty feed company thermometer on the back porch. It had been mounted in its corner for as long as she could remember, but had always been accurate. Gingerly, she fingered the tip of her nose. It was pink with sunburn and dusted with a few new freckles. She would have to remember the sunscreen tomorrow.

As the shadows grew longer and the temperature became more comfortable, Elizabeth decided to look for the old hen and go back and poke around the old lock once again. She was still curious about the events of the day before and thought it would be interesting to see how far down the towpath she could hike.

The biddy must have been out hunting for grasshoppers, because Elizabeth didn't see or hear her. In the morning, she would check all the places the hens used to like to hide, but at the moment she was in a hurry to get back over to the lock. She wanted to investigate further.

Trailed by Forsooth, Elizabeth waded through tall grasses and weeds. Even though the sun was beginning its evening descent, heat still shimmered over the land. She gained the top of the earthen embankment. From there she could see distant woods dissolving into blue evening haze. The slanting sun splashed amber light over the surrounding fields of tasseled corn and ripening soybeans. The water in the canal was as flat and motionless as green mirror. Slapping a large mosquito behind her knee and waving off a zooming horsefly, Elizabeth hiked toward the heap of fallen stone blocks and the place where the thicket of willows obscured the path.

The wind hit her just as she started to scramble over a mossy slab. Elizabeth froze to the spot as it wrapped itself around her like a living being. She shivered in its bitter grasp. Once again a veil of mist, unaffected by the screaming gale, rose upward, twining snake-line around her body. All was disappearing from sight as the fog swelled around her.

Caught in the keening blast were the sounds from the night before: muffled voices, splashing, the trumpeting horn. But now, all were growing louder and more distinct!

Over it all rose the same singsong from before: "Hey-ey-ey-ey! Lo-o-o-ock!"

Then, from the low-hanging trees just a few yards in front of Elizabeth, with an explosion of leaves, twigs and flying clods of mud, crashed a team of mules! A stocky, bearded man, clad in shabby, greasy-looking clothing, tromped beside the harnessed animals. With a lift of his scruffy chin and a baleful glare at Elizabeth, he aimed and spat a brown stream of tobacco juice into the canal. Nodding with satisfaction at the liquid plop, he dug around in his filthy shirt, located a wad of the vile stuff, bit off a sizable chunk with the few teeth visible in his mouth and with his tongue, tucked it comfortably into his cheek, all without breaking stride.

CHAPTER 6

"Hey! Girlie! Outta the way!" the teamster barked.

Startled, Elizabeth leaped aside. Dazed, she stared as the team and driver plodded methodically by.

The muleskinner grunted at her as he passed. "Ya better be watchin' yer step! 'N git yer gear offa the path!"

Elizabeth shook her head slightly to clear it. It must be a dream again; it was so real though! She could smell the mules' sweaty coats and the rank body odor of their driver. She could hear the flies buzzing around the team's long ears and...*and the creak and jingle of their leather harness...*

What had he said to her? Her gear? The stunned woman looked down and saw a large trunk and a flowered carpetbag. Suddenly weak, she sank down onto the sturdy, wooden chest. Her heart was pounding as if it would burst from her chest. She put both hands to her breast in an effort to calm the frenzied beating. She was going to faint! She couldn't get her breath and the buzzing of the mules' flies had grown louder and angrier and she felt as if the noise originated from within her head. The sky and earth skidded around her. She bent to put her head between her knees in a last-ditch effort to remain conscious. She immediately jolted upright. *Boots. She was wearing boots.* She turned her feet this way and that. Weird, pointy-toed boots with a line of tiny buttons running up the outside had replaced her white canvas sneakers.

The jean shorts and T-shirt were gone, too. A tight-fitting dress cinched her from ribs to hips and made it difficult to breathe and impossible to put her head between her knees. A long skirt billowed down over her boot tops. She twisted about, pulling and tugging at the fabric, trying to ascertain if it were real. *Gloves.* Delicate white lace gloves. In order to beat down the panic that was closing her throat, she squeezed her eyes shut, took a tremulous cleansing breath in through her nose, exhaled it out through her mouth and gave her head another shake to clear her sight and her mind. With the toss of her head, she felt an unfamiliar weight and slowly raised both hands to her head and found...*a hat.* Not a normal hat like she might jam on to go hiking, but a woven straw bonnet, adorned with flowers and two yellow ribbons that tied under her chin.

That did it.

"Time to wake up now," she said aloud, willing herself to exit from a dream that was beginning to take on nightmare proportions. Because if this wasn't a dream, she had plunged over the edge of sanity into...into what?

"Hoo-oo-oot! Hoo-oo-oot! Hoo-oo-oot" A horn blared and a fine tenor voice sang out, "Hey-ey-ey! Lo-o-ock!"

Elizabeth jumped up off the trunk.

Staggering at the impact she stared as the long rope attached to the mules that had just passed by dipped into the canal briefly, then rose again. Her eyes followed the rope to the amazing sight of a boat, a *canal boat!* She stared as it drew even and glided slowly by. The long, low-riding vessel was constructed of wood and painted white with red trim. There were two small cabins at each end of the craft. Curtains fluttered from windows replete with green shutters. The large open area in the center of the ship was stacked high with crates and barrels. A man in old-fashioned clothing, equally as soiled as the gruff character with the mules, stood atop the little house at the rear. He leaned slightly on a large pole that was parallel with the deck. It was attached to a rudder at the water line. The steersman politely touched his hat to Elizabeth as the craft passed so closely she could have touched it with an outstretched hand.

As it floated on down the canal, Elizabeth read "*Cincinnati Belle*" arching in ornate script across the back of the boat. The startled woman took a step back as she regained her senses. The Miami and Erie Canal was full of water up and down as far as she could see, even the junction with the Wabash and Erie was full. She had only seen water clear to the junction once, during a bad spring flood when she was a child. As she turned slowly around, taking in her surroundings, her heart flipped in alarm and her hands flew to her mouth as she gasped.

Suddenly, the clamor, sights and smells of a bustling village crowded her senses. She was standing in the middle of a rustic, yet busy little town that stood in a large clearing. Dense forest surrounded the settlement. Wood smoke hung in the air. Chickens squawked. She turned toward a clanging sound and saw a well-muscled blacksmith in a filthy leather apron rhythmically at work. Horse and mule drawn wagons trundled. Three canal boats, laden with people, supplies and extra mules, plied the waters of the much-widened canals, jockeying for a place to dock. Scattered along narrow dirt lanes were log cabins and small frame houses. Several more dwellings were in various stages of construction.

A laughing group of children ran up with an entourage of barking dogs chasing behind. They slowed slightly to stare at the strange woman, then ran on down the dusty street. A small clapboard church with a stubby steeple stood apart from the other buildings.

Frantically, Elizabeth spun around. Where was she? She needed to get her bearings. Everything was changed.

"That must be her! Halloo! Halloo!"

"Elizabeth? Elizabeth Hudson?"

"We're coming!"

"The *Cincinnati Belle* musta come in earlier n' usual."

Elizabeth woodenly inched around, afraid of what she might see next. Coming toward her was a group of four people. In front were a large bearded man and a short plump woman, apparently his wife. Her smile beamed out from under a jaunty straw bonnet. Behind them was another couple who appeared to be slightly younger than herself. He looked to be a blond version of the older man, while the young woman was dark haired and smiling shyly.

Elizabeth quickly turned and checked behind her to see if they were talking to someone else, but she stood alone on the towpath. She smiled weakly before being smothered in a tight embrace that knocked her bonnet askew. The woman held her at arms' length.

"William! There's no denying she's a Hudson!" Another hug. "We've been watching the packets for days, just waiting for your arrival…and here you are! Safe and sound! Travel is so hard on a body, isn't it Rachel?" Rachel, the younger woman, was not given a chance to reply. "Imagine!" the perky woman continued. "Coming the entire way from Cincinnati all by yourself!"

The larger, bearded man patted the top of a stone monument set in the ground. The numbers 181 were etched into it. "One hundred and eighty-one miles exactly, there's your proof!"

"Land! All that way in only a week's time, and in 1850, too! Just to think that I would live to see the day of such wonders."

"Next thing you know, Ma, we'll be traveling to the moon!" the young man teased his mother.

All four laughed merrily, while Elizabeth managed a feeble smile.

1850! "*Eighteen hundred and fifty?* Her mouth went dry and the dizziness threatened again.

The younger of the two women did not interrupt the other while she was greeting Elizabeth, but simply nodded with a gentle smile.

"Elizabeth, I am your uncle, William Hudson, your father's brother, you know. This is your Aunt Ruth, and your cousin Caleb.

Hudson, same name, but I sure don't remember any of these people at any family reunion, Elizabeth thought.

"And this young lady is Miss Rachel White," the older man continued, "Caleb's intended."

Rachel put her hand on Elizabeth's arm. "I am so happy to meet you! I just know we shall be great friends." Taking a closer look at the perspiration beading Elizabeth's face, she asked, "Are you feeling poorly? You look a mite peaked!"

"Why she does at that!" Aunt Ruth broke in with alarm. "Do ye ail, child?"

"I-I-I," Elizabeth croaked. To her amazement, her voice

worked. "I'm fine," she stuttered, dabbing shakily at her forehead and upper lip with the handkerchief Rachel had pressed into her hand.

"Well, let's not stand out here in the hot sun jawin' all day, Mother. I'll wager that welcome feast of yours is nye onto ready by now!" Caleb hoisted the heavy wooden trunk with very little effort and headed toward the settlement.

Uncle William collected the carpetbag and Aunt Ruth bustled after Caleb chattering instructions for the care of the trunk.

Rachel smiled warmly at Elizabeth. "Thank you so much for coming to stay for a while and help with our wedding!"

She took Elizabeth lightly by the elbow with a lace-mitted hand. The two younger women fell in line and followed the procession.

CHAPTER 7

As Elizabeth allowed herself to be led away from the canal, she took in her surroundings with awe. Nothing was the same as it had been just a few minutes before. At least, she thought only a short amount of time had passed. She wasn't sure of anything at the moment. She noticed with amazement that what had been a stifling, humid evening was now a cool, clear morning. The wide-open fields of her family's farm were gone. In their place were trees - tall, massive and so numerous they hemmed the little settlement in on all sides, the foliage splashed here and there with the bright tints of autumn. Only the canals and several dusty tracks served as openings in the dense forest.

The jumble of stone blocks was gone, restored into a working lock. At that very moment, The *Cincinnati Belle* was slowly sinking out of sight behind the massive wooden gates of the lock, preparing to emerge at a lower elevation. From a small house beside the canal a portly man made his appearance at the blare of the boat's horn. He was busily shouting orders and operating the lock.

Elizabeth's mind raced, casting frantically about for an explanation, as they proceeded down a path and away from the canal. Was she still in the big white bed dreaming? Did she fall, hitting her head? Was she having some sort of hallucination or seizure?

The older woman was asking her a question.

"I-I'm sorry, I didn't hear you."

"Poor lamb! I suppose you are exhausted! I was just asking after your family."

"Oh, they…uh…were fine, when I…um…left." Elizabeth faltered.

"And your grandmother?"

"Oh, she's fine, fine…"

The older woman cleared her throat and spoke carefully.

"Elizabeth, dear, we were so sorry to hear of your husband's passing. Such a sad thing, and so young, too. Your mother wrote of how dutifully you nursed him." She sighed. "When a doctor insists on treating those afflicted with contagion, he risks his own life."

Elizabeth struggled for a reply. "Yes, yes…thank you."

"Well, now!" Aunt Ruth declared briskly. "We'll get you home and get some decent victuals into you and then you may rest until you are all recovered from your journey. It must have been quite uncomfortable at times, squeezed in with all those other passengers, strangers and all. Still, your mother assured us that you are a capable young lady."

Rachel, the younger woman, spoke. "I hope you find your room to your liking. Mother Ruth and I had a wonderful time fixing it for you. I'm sure it's not as elegant as you are accustomed to, but it *is* right next to mine! Caleb lives out on our place…well, it will be our place after we're married." She blushed. "I only arrived a year ago, but already I feel as if Junction is my home."

"Junction!" The word exploded in Elizabeth's mind so that for a brief moment she was afraid she had uttered the word aloud.

Aunt Ruth smiled and said: "Rachel come west to teach school, but our Caleb won her over. I'll have myself a new daughter, but Junction will have to find another school m'arm!"

They were in front of a brick house now. Was this the Old Brick? She stopped suddenly and peered up at the paned windows. It didn't look much like the one she knew, but there was no denying the simple, classic lines of the Federal structure. The porch, although unpainted, was scrubbed smooth and clean.

The Hudsons entered the home through a door that opened into the kitchen, which bore little resemblance to the room in which Elizabeth had spent so many hours. The fireplace was the same, only clean and bright, the edges of the bricks sharp and new. Embers glowed on the hearth, warming several pots that hung from iron cranes. There was no stove or other appliance anywhere, only black iron pots, pans and wooden utensil hanging about on crude hooks.

Aunt Ruth removed her bonnet and disappeared into another room, talking over her shoulder as she went. "I'll be right back, this is my good bonnet and I want to put it back in its box. I only wear it to meeting and for special."

She bustled back into the room, tying an apron over her full skirt. Lifting the lid off a steaming pot hanging on an iron crane over the coals, she stirred the contents with a long handled wooden spoon. A delicious aroma filled the room. "Rachel, Father and Caleb have taken Elizabeth's things to her room. Why don't you help her get settled while I take up the dinner? It'll be ready soon."

"I would be happy to help you unpack, Elizabeth," Rachel offered with a shy smile. She led the way through the main room of the house and up the steps.

All seemed familiar, yet strange. Some features of the home, such as the walnut woodwork and built-in cupboards, remained the same. The windows, although in the same locations, were different. Small, individual panes of bubbly, green tinted glass filled the opening.

Elizabeth found maneuvering the narrow steps in a long skirt a challenge and tripped twice as she followed Rachel.

Upstairs were the same low ceilings and the sun streamed in the window from the hall just as it had always done every morning Elizabeth had awakened in her grandparents' house. Rachel led Elizabeth into her very own bedroom. The faded paper was gone, replaced by rough plaster walls.

"We have the entire upper story to ourselves," Rachel explained as she untied the ribbons on her bonnet. "You have Caleb's old room and I have Mother and Father Hudson's. When Caleb and I decided to marry, he built a new cabin out on our farm and his parents moved downstairs so I could live here. That way, I can save my wages from teaching to help us set up housekeeping."

"We so enjoyed readying the room. Does it suit you?"

"Oh, yes. It's fine…lovely, really lovely."

A rustic bed was situated in a corner of the room. A large

plump feather mattress rested on criss-crossed ropes instead of box springs. It was covered in a patchwork quilt of bright blues and yellows. A fat pillow, in a crisply ironed pillowcase, rested at the head of the bed. On the wide floorboards was a thick, oval braided rug. It was colorful and added to the clean cheerfulness of the room. On the walls above the bed and simple oak dresser were several small, framed landscapes. Elizabeth stepped around her trunk to take a closer look.

The paintings were watercolors that picked up the clear hues of wildflowers and deep shade of the trees shadowing the Auglaize River. In all three, the artist had captured the glow of sunlight on the countryside. There was nothing amateur about the work. The light hand with color and the attention to light reminded her of the American Impressionist school of art.

"These are really nice, very well done!"

"Thank you, I did them just for you." Rachel beamed at the compliment.

Astonished, Elizabeth turned. "You painted these?"

"Yes, a silly hobby for a woman about to be married, isn't it? I should be spending my time observing Mother Ruth in the kitchen, learning how to make Caleb's favorite dishes." The dark haired young woman admitted with a rueful smile. "I love to paint, though. Sometimes I see something, well, I sort of see and I feel it at the same time. If I cannot put it down in a sketch or with paint, I feel as if I'm missing something, forgetting an important message for someone." She stared at the floor, embarrassed by her confession.

Elizabeth nodded in understanding. "I don't think there is anything silly about your paintings. They're are wonderful. Have you ever tried selling any of your work?"

Rachel was shocked. "Oh no. A lady wouldn't sell her paintings. It wouldn't be proper. For a church bazaar, perhaps, but not to earn a living." She sighed, "Besides, who would want to buy the dabblings of a school teacher?"

"Well, I suppose I should leave you to freshen up before dinner," she said briskly. "I can help you unpack later, if you wish.

Fresh water and a towel are on the washstand over there. I'll go help Aunt Ruth. Just come down when you are ready."

Elizabeth smiled stiffly until the rustle of Rachel's skirts faded, then sank down onto the bed, removed the straw bonnet, rested her head in her hands and squeezed her eyes shut. "Wake up! Wake up! Wake up!" she muttered through gritted teeth, pounding on her thighs with her fists. She willed herself to rise up out of the most realistic nightmare that had ever invaded her dreams.

"Elizabeth!" a voice called.

She jerked her head up hopefully.

"Dinner's ready!" Aunt Ruth called from below.

Defeated, Elizabeth struggled out of the deep hollow she had made in the featherbed and made her way over to the washstand. Leaning on one hand, she scooped water and splashed it onto her flushed cheeks with the other. Then she scrubbed hurriedly at her face with the thin piece of flannel. Taking a comb from the dresser top, she ran it through her curly hair, straightened her clothing and walked slowly toward the door. Taking a deep breath, Elizabeth tried to reassure herself. She couldn't be stuck in 1850 forever.

CHAPTER 8

Elizabeth adapted very quickly to life in the busy little town of Junction in the year 1850. Although she did not forget her present day life completely, it was as if a gauze veil was pulled over the memories and emotions attached to her world. Memory of her modern existence grew distant and vague as she was immersed in the past. As each day drew to a close, it became more difficult to determine which was real: her past or this present.

The Hudsons of 1850 were warm and loving and Elizabeth felt very much a part of the family. September whirled into October as she adapted to the rhythm and the rigors of mid-nineteenth century daily life and the many social customs and gender expectations that were observed.

Preparations for Rachel and Caleb's wedding, although quite simple by modern standards, were elaborate for the day. Especially since Rachel, at the age of twenty-four was considered practically an old maid.

One crisp morning early in October, Rachel gently shook Elizabeth awake. "Elizabeth! Wake up!" She plopped, in a very un-teacherlike manner, on Elizabeth's feet, still snug under a couple of Aunt Ruth's ample quilts. "Father Hudson just came back from town and says a new shipment of dry goods for Cunningham's is at the dock! They're unloading it now!"

Elizabeth squinted against the bright morning light with one eye. "I thought you were a city girl, how can you be so cheerful this early in the morning?"

Rachel bounced. "I already let you sleep much later than usual. Look, it's full sun up!"

"Oh, so that's what's searing my eyeballs. It's daylight," retorted Elizabeth sarcastically.

You know you promised to help me choose the cloth for my wedding dress! Wake up!" Rachel yanked the covers back.

“I’m up! I’m up!” Elizabeth groaned, flinging her arm over her eyes to shield them from the glare.

The women had decided that the shopping trip was occasion enough to don some of their best attire. Elizabeth stood in her room deciding what to wear. If the wardrobe that had been encased in the large wooden trunk was any indication, her “family” in Cincinnati was quite well to do. The many garments were constructed by hand with exquisite attention to detail and workmanship. Elizabeth discovered that becoming accustomed to the elaborate female costume of the day took some effort. Even everyday dress involved many layers.

First was a thin, white cotton slip called a “chemise.” Long, loose pants or “pantalets” of the same fabric accompanied the chemise. Aunt Ruth usually referred to these two garments as a “shimmy” and “drawers.” They were trimmed with layers and layers of intricate handmade lace. Over the shimmy went Elizabeth’s least favorite garment: the corset. It was a vest-like garment with many tiny pockets, in which were inserted little whalebone slivers, called stays. She shuddered to think that a whale had given its life to be made into underwear. Elizabeth found it nearly impossible to take a deep breath once stuffed inside and the laces were drawn. Fearing the ill effects it might have on her body, she didn’t cinch herself in nearly as tight as was the fashion. She felt that corsets were ridiculous garments and avoided them whenever possible.

Over the corset went a corset cover, much like a camisole. Then came layers of petticoats, which were essential to make skirts stand out fashionably. In cooler weather, one donned a flannel petticoat first, followed by another with at least three tiers or flounces stiffened with starch. On top of this went another petticoat for every day, and even more for fancier occasions. Elizabeth feared that she would suffocate under the piles of clothing, but as the days grew colder and she discovered that heat in the house was spotty at best, she grew thankful for the insulating layers.

Aunt Ruth had a woman come in to help with laundry and

ironing. Uncle William was a fairly well to do landowner. This explained how he could afford a fine home like the brick house and the hired help for household chores. Elizabeth was glad for herself. She did not relish the thought of standing over an ironing board with the clumsy cast irons, toiling over every ruffle and tuck.

Rachel tapped lightly on the door and popped her head into the room. "Are you having difficulty selecting a costume?" she inquired. "May I be of assistance? You have the prettiest clothes I've seen since I left Cleveland. Conditions *are* a little rugged out here," she confessed.

"Oh, sure, yes, that would be nice."

Rachel peered at the dresses lying folded in tissue in the trunk. "I think this apple green silk. It will complement your complexion!" She withdrew it from the trunk and shook it carefully to dislodge the wrinkles. Little lace packets tumbled out of the folds and a faint scent of dried lavender rose from the glossy fabric. "Look at those dear little sachets, did you make them?"

"No." Elizabeth answered with all honesty. "I never have been too good with a needle…she paused as she remembered her vocation and smiled, "and thread."

"There must be a bonnet, too." Rachel stated.

"Yes, there's one in there somewhere. You'll have to help me tie it on, because if you don't, it will be hanging off one ear by the time I reach the bottom of the steps!"

"Oh the wonderful things in your trunk make me long for Cleveland. Being a port city, there were always new shipments of wonderful things," the petite young woman reminisced. There were so many parties and balls back home. I thought I wanted adventure and was bored with such things, but every once in a while…" her voice trailed off. Then her blue eyes brightened. "I would much rather go to a husking bee with Caleb, though!"

Rachel helped arrange her new friend's auburn hair into a becoming, popular style. It was parted in the middle with three ringlets arranged over each ear. Although she felt silly, she accepted the new coif, as she had no wish to stand out.

Down in the kitchen Aunt Ruth smiled up at the ceiling at the muffled sounds of conversation. It was so good to have young people in the house. They added so much life! Rachel and Elizabeth were good friends already. Caleb good-naturedly joked about "Belle," his nickname for Elizabeth, after the *"Cincinnati Belle"* canal packet on which she had arrived.

Ruth Hudson mused to herself while stirring a pot of oatmeal porridge. Elizabeth was a bright young woman, though she did have some strange ways. She was a mite outspoken with her opinions for a female and a little clumsy with some of the household duties. For a city girl, she surely knew her way around a barnyard and was a willing worker, throwing herself into any task assigned and finding plenty on her own.

Thumping on the back porch announced the arrival of Caleb for breakfast. Though living out on his own farm, he still helped his father do the chores on the home place and took his meals in his mother's bountiful kitchen. Before entering the house, the young man pulled his boots off by the heels with the help of the wooden jack, always present on the porch floor. Well before sunup he had toted water for washing and cooking. It was quite cold in the early October air. Using a tin basin, he washed quickly, shivering as the icy drops splashed over his face and neck. Winter was not far off, but right now the autumn sunshine spilled clear and golden through the open door onto the spotless painted floor of the kitchen.

Caleb sat at the table just as Elizabeth and Rachel swept into the room. Breakfast was simple fare and over quickly. Rachel and Ruth cleaned up the house while Elizabeth volunteered to tend to the poultry.

Elizabeth didn't really care all that much for chickens, but thought that Rachel would appreciate the opportunity to keep her boots clean. The main reason Elizabeth avoided the hen house was a nasty old rooster she had dubbed "Colonel Sanders." He never missed a chance to fly at her. He pecked at her ankles, backing off and flapping in again and again so that it appeared the two of them were engaged in some sort of awkward dance around the barnyard. As she dodged each new onslaught, corn from her basket showered to the ground, much to the hens' delight. She dispatched the chore as quickly as possible and picked her way back to the house trying to avoid dirtying her boots. Grumbling under her breath, Elizabeth picked feathers and kernels of corn off her clothing and out of her hair as she went. She maliciously hoped the old bird ended up in a stew, and soon!

CHAPTER 9

The Cunningham Dry Goods Emporium was not nearly as grand as its name implied. It was a simple log structure with a brick facade. Like many of the merchants in Junction, the Cunninghams conducted business from the front half of the building and lived in the back. Adelia Cunningham promised her customers only the finest merchandise available. Although wealthy clientele in Junction was limited, she wanted to be sure that their business came her way. The tall, buxom woman of regal bearing was always impeccable in manners and dress. She perused her Godey's Ladies' Book vigilantly and took great pains to replicate the fashions from "back East" for her own wardrobe.

When the Hudson women arrived, the proprietress was sorting through the new shipment. She greeted them with a genuine smile, excited about the opportunity to offer advice about suitable fabrics, patterns and trims. The fact that the popular schoolmistress' wedding would have half the town in attendance noting every detail of her gown had not escaped Adelia Cunningham.

She swept across the room to greet them. "Good Morning! Good Morning!" she warbled. Isn't it a beautiful day? But not one bit more lovely than our bride-to-be!" She took Rachel's gloved hands into her own, pumping them up and down with each syllable. "My dear, you are simply glowing! Isn't she simply glowing, Mrs. Hudson?"

Not waiting for a reply, she took Rachel by the arm and escorted the young lady to the pile of material bolts. "Mr. Cunningham is down at the wharf, so we're not all unpacked yet, perhaps you would like to observe while I finish? It will be a little like Christmas!" The older woman gushed.

Ruth Hudson, had never been woman to stand on ceremony when there was work to be done. "Adelia Cunningham," she said, as she removed her wraps. "It's a sin for three able-bodied women to watch another work. We'll help," she said, determinedly.

Everyone busied herself removing the cheesecloth outer wrapping from the bolts while Mrs. Cunningham kept track of her new inventory in a leather bound ledger. An hour passed swiftly as the women sorted and compared, holding various selections up to Rachel to find those that enhanced her hair color and complexion.

Rachel's family in Cleveland was comfortably well off. Her father was a noted attorney and her older brother had recently joined his partnership. Therefore, Rachel's wedding gown would be of finer stuff than most. In 1850, a wedding dress would be worn for years. No woman along the Miami and Erie Canal could afford to wear a dress only once. Often, it would be thin and faded before being made over into children's clothing. The smallest scraps were eventually fitted into a quilt or rag rug. Nothing went to waste.

The door of the shop squeaked open and three young girls entered, chattering among themselves. Their conversation stopped in mid-giggle when they observed the adults in the room. There was a slight pause, and then the group rushed up to Rachel.

"Miss White! Miss White!"

"Why, hello, Alice, Mary, Katherine! How good it is to see you!" Rachel obviously held affection for the girls as she lovingly placed her hands on their shoulders. Elizabeth estimated their ages at about twelve or thirteen, placing the youngest of the three, Katherine, around ten or eleven. Mary and Katherine were obviously sisters, with their hazel eyes and blond frizzy curls. Alice, the tallest of the three, had golden brown eyes, a sprinkle of freckles across her nose and braids, much the same color as Elizabeth's russet hair.

"Elizabeth, I would like you to meet my star pupils," Rachel said. "This is Alice Ayres and the O'Dillon sisters, Mary and Katherine. Girls, this is Mrs. Elizabeth Hudson-Scott lately come of Cincinnati."

The young girls shyly made their acquaintance with

Elizabeth.

Katherine, was the youngest and least reticent of the group. Her hazel eyes sparkled as she piped, "We knew you was here, but Ma said she needed to come by to visit proper afore we could come to see you." Without pausing for breath, she opened her hand and proudly displayed a coin. "Ma needs a new packet of pins. I got to carry the money this time! Charlie had to stay home and do chores!" she finished triumphantly.

"Charlie is our younger brother, he's six and sticks like burr," Mary explained soberly.

Alice Ayres spoke up. "My father went to school in Cincinnati to be a doctor, Mrs. Scott. He says your husband was a classmate and a really good physician…"

Elizabeth stiffened at the news that someone in Junction actually knew the person who was reported to be her late husband.

"And…and…" Alice's face flooded with color, interpreting Elizabeth's reaction as one of grief. "I'm sorry," she whispered and lapsed into an embarrassed silence.

"Oh…no, that's quite all right, Alice!" Elizabeth covered quickly. "I think it's a fine thing, that…what your father said," she reassured the child, fervently hoping there was no one else in Junction, other than the Hudsons, actually acquainted with her "family" in Cincinnati. Elizabeth avoided conversation about Cincinnati, letting her hosts believe her delicacy toward the subject was the reaction of a grieving widow.

"The new term starts tomorrow, does it not?" Rachel broke in and asked her admirers.

"Yes." Katherine wrinkled her nose. "But I don't want to go! The new schoolmaster looks like…like…" She cast about for an apt description, until her glance landed on a large barrel in the corner that emanated strong fumes of vinegar and dill. She brightened. "He looks like a *pickle*!"

Mary was aghast at her sister's audacity. "*Katherine*!"

"Well, he does!"

Rachel, while attempting to smooth the situation, found it

difficult to hide her smile. "I am sure that Master Reed has your best interests at heart, Katherine."

Alice leaned over, and in a loud whisper, confided to the younger girl. "I think he looks like a pickle, too!"

Mary glared at her best friend. "Alice, you're no better!"

Her school teaching skills still sharp, Rachel quickly changed the subject in order to avoid further discord. "Young ladies, she said briskly, "you are here just in time to help me choose the fabric for the dress in which I am to be wed!"

The three were speechless at the honor. And, although there was a wide range of opinions, soon all were in agreement over a heavy, embroidered satin. On creamy ground, pink rosebuds and blue forget-me-nots danced among twining leaves of green ivy. Mrs. Cunningham draped a fold of the luxurious cloth over Rachel's shoulder. The sheen of the rich fabric glowed against the young woman's pale skin and dark hair.

"The rosebuds are the same hue as your blushing cheeks and the forget-me-nots mirror the sapphire of your eyes," she said.

Elizabeth fought the urge to roll her own eyes at the woman's syrupy manner, but seeing the expression of excitement on Rachel's delicate face, controlled herself.

"Do you really think this one looks best? Mother Ruth? Elizabeth?" Rachel's cheeks were crimson from all the attention.

"Oh, Miss White, it's beautiful!" Alice Ayres clasped her hands together.

Mary sighed, "Oh I hope I'll be as pretty a bride as you, Miss White."

It was agreed that the satin was an excellent choice. Mrs. Cunningham hummed gaily as she measured out fifteen yards of the most expensive cloth they had ever stocked at the emporium. Mr. Cunningham had argued against it, but Adelia's gamble had paid. She knew when she selected it, that the glossy yardage would be perfect for Rachel's wedding.

CHAPTER 10

"Ouch!" Elizabeth struggled and won over the urge to add an expletive. She sucked on her bleeding index finger. Her skill and patience with sewing were identical: short. Exasperated, she dropped the tangled wad of thread into her lap and looked helplessly from Aunt Ruth to Rachel.

"Sorry," she said sheepishly.

The two other women exchanged looks.

"Oh dear," Aunt Ruth said, theatrically, "I'm going to run out of thread any moment now! Elizabeth, would it be too much of an imposition for you to trot into town and run a few errands?"

"Ready," Elizabeth said, scrambling out of her chair and throwing a shawl over her shoulders. She was at the door with a basket over her arm before Ruth Hudson finished scratching a list on a tiny scrap of brown paper with her quill pen.

"Now, how is it," Ruth asked as she watched through the glass as her niece walked briskly toward town, "that a woman, a lady with a fancy city upbringing and a finishing school education can hardly sew a stitch worthy of a flour sack?"

"Elizabeth's talents just lie elsewhere, Mother Ruth," Rachel replied.

Elizabeth's relief at being out of the house and into the brisk autumn air far outweighed her embarrassment at not being much help with the needlework on Rachel's wedding dress and trousseau. Always athletic, it felt good to stretch her muscles and she worked the kinks that had insidiously taken up residence in the small of her back during the hours she had spent bent over the interminable stitching. As soon as the brick house was out of sight, she took Aunt Ruth's suggestion literally and picked up her pace, trotting as fast as her voluminous garments would allow.

Elizabeth had adhered to a rigorous workout schedule with an almost religious fervor in her modern-day life. It had abruptly come to an end with her trip through time, and even in conjunction with a daily diet that relied heavily on animal fats, her physique had remained trim. She marveled at the sheer amount of physical labor that was required to clothe people and keep them sheltered and fed in 1850. The work was endless. Aunt Ruth and Rachel never sat down without picking up some sort of handiwork, be it patchwork, quilting or mending. Although recreation enabled people opportunities to socialize, it was also devised to ease the amount of time spent on necessary toil: quilting and husking bees and barn raisings.

Elizabeth skirted around the numerous saloons. They varied from taverns as pleasant and clean as the Cunningham store, to humble log lean-tos with a board slung across two stumps, an earthenware jug and a couple of dented tin mugs. At any hour of day or night, a crowd of canal workers and muleskinners and other rough customers could be found gathered around such establishments. She passed the noisy sawmill, several inns, the town's two blacksmiths and the brewery, with its yeasty odor. A new brick Catholic Church was under construction. Junction was definitely a progressive settlement.

After Elizabeth collected the few sundries Aunt Ruth had requested from Watson's General Store, she followed along the canal for the short walk home. She found the passenger packets and cargo boats plying the waters of the Miami and Erie Canal fascinating. Although it was purported that she had arrived in such a manner, she had not experienced travel on the smooth waters.

Shouted orders of captains and mule drivers floated in the October air. On board, the captains' wives called to each other while going about daily housekeeping. Laundry flapped in the cool breeze, while children scampered up and down the decks, in and out of damp sheets and the legs of long underwear, or as Aunt Ruth referred to them, "woolens."

As Elizabeth approached the path to the brick house, a man leaped from a canal boat landing lightly on his toes in front of her. She started and almost dropped her brown paper wrapped package.

"Grand afternoon, tisn't it, ma'am?" He bowed slightly as he swept a tall battered beaver hat from his head. His hair, straight, black and glossy as ink, fell over his forehead. "So this is the "Cincinnati Belle" I've heard tell so much about!" He rested his work-callused hands on his hips and leaned back. With his coffee-brown eyes twinkling, he said, "I can see why."

Elizabeth's freckles disappeared as redness rushed up her neck and into her face. She had never thought of herself as any kind of beauty.

"There now, I've embarrassed you. Mores the shame. I'm a cad, there's no argument there" he said ruefully. Brightening, he said, "Allow me to introduce myself proper: Daniel Mahafy, pilot of the "*Wabash Queene*," long-time friend of Caleb Hudson."

"Oh! Yes, *Daniel.* Hello. Caleb and Rachel have often spoken of you!" Elizabeth relaxed a little and the heat of her blush dissipated.

"Perhaps I should have waited for a formal introduction, in order to be proper," he said, still castigating himself for what he apparently considered to be a dreadful social faux pas.

Elizabeth, who thought she detected a slight brogue in his speech, couldn't stand to seem him heap abuse upon himself any longer. "No need to stand on ceremony, Mr. Mahafy. I'm Elizabeth Hudson-Scott and I'm most happy to make your acquaintance."

"Caleb and I have been friends for quite a while. We tormented a more than a few schoolmasters in our day. When I put up for the winter in Junction we get to visit a bit."

Elizabeth remembered the bundle under her arm. "I had better hurry along with this. Are you planning on attending the wedding, Mr. Mahafy?" She asked, self-conscious of the hopeful tone in her voice and suddenly aware of the fact that her speech was beginning to take on the more formal stilted style of the day.

The boatman grinned and flipped his hat back onto his head. "I'll be there, with bells on, Mrs. Scott."

Elizabeth continued along the canal, smiling and feeling very youthful as a result of Captain Mahafy's attention. The dark-eyed captain leaped nimbly back onto his craft and strode along the catwalk between the cabin in the middle of the ship, which stabled the mules, to the fore cabin, matching his pace to hers. Resuming his work, he lifted a heavily laden cloth sack and hefted it to his ample shoulder.

"Mrs. Scott," he called after her.

She stopped and turned.

He thumped the bag to the deck and dusted the chaff from his hands. "I know there are proper ways to do this. I don't have the time to prance and mince about it. Might I come to call? Would you walk out with me some Sunday?"

"I would be delighted, Mr. Mahafy."

* * * *

True to his statement about not being prone to shilly-shallying, Daniel Mahafy knocked on the parlor door of the Hudson home the very next Sunday. Elizabeth, also of a straightforward nature, had donned her apple green silk and was waiting for him.

Indian Summer washed the countryside with a golden light and balmy temperatures. A stiff breeze kept the mosquito population at bay, so that walking along the narrow path that had been cleared by the river was no longer a torment, but a pleasant occupation.

Daniel was an entertaining conversationalist and Elizabeth found his tales of growing up as a "canal rat" fascinating.

"My father come to America from Ireland when he heard they were seeking workers to help build the Erie Canal," he said. Again Elizabeth detected the slightest brogue when he pronounced "heard" as "hard." She found it endearing.

"My mother stayed behind with all my brothers and sisters until my father saved enough to send for them." Daniel picked up her left hand with his and placed it on his right arm. Elizabeth, who had always opened her own doors, let it rest there.

"He found work in New York State, then sent for Mum and the rest. I hadn't come along yet," he grinned at her. "You know they say the best is always last."

"Well, most of them were grown and gone off with families of their own by the time my Pa saved up enough to build a boat of his own." He paused a moment, reflecting. My father wasn't like a lot of them canalers. He was careful with his pay packet, it wasn't much, but he didn't spend it on the drink, like so many of them aim to do. With the opening of the canals in eastern Ohio, we moved west. My father, Patrick his name was, procured his own packet and provided a good living, transporting people and shipping goods."

He stopped suddenly and pointed at porcelain sky, where a bald eagle circled above the shallow, slow moving river. As they watched, the magnificent bird swooped down, it's talons splashing into the water. Then it lifted away from the river with a few powerful beats of its wings and disappeared over the trees.

"The sun is going down, I must get back and help get supper on," Elizabeth said reluctantly.

They turned around and headed back over the recently harvested fields to the house. For a while, they walked in companionable silence. Daniel broke into a whistle. It was a sweet, mournful tune.

"I've never heard that song. What's the name of it," she asked.

"I'm not really sure of the name, just one I picked up over the years," he said. "From the time I was old enough to ride on the back of a mule, I rode up there. At night, Pa would have me sing so's he'd know if I'd fallen asleep and unbeknownst to him, toppled off of ol' Charity and into the drink and drowned," he chuckled.

That evening as Elizabeth readied for bed, she found herself humming the tune that Daniel whistled on their way home from the river. She had just blown out the candle when Rachel called from her room across the narrow hall.

"Elizabeth?"

"Yes?"

"How was your walk with Daniel? He certainly had an appetite at supper, didn't he? You must have walked a fair piece. Fresh air will make one quite hungry."

"Well, Rachel," Elizabeth replied, grinning in the dark. "Which question do you want me to answer first?" Not waiting for a reply, she said, "With no previous experience as to Captain Mahafy's appetites, I would venture to say that, yes, he seemed to have a good one. As for how far we walked, you are right, it was "a fair piece."

She smothered her laughter in a pillow at the silence emanating from the room across the hall.

After a moment Rachel spoke again and this time there was laughter in her voice. "Very well, I deserved that. It's just that he seems so taken with you. Caleb says he's known Daniel ever since he can remember and he's never known anyone to turn his head quite as you have."

This time it was Elizabeth who was silent. To listen to his talk, Daniel neither knew nor wished for any other lifestyle. Never married, the rollicking life on the Miami and Erie was his mate.

CHAPTER 11

The glitter of autumn's first hard frost greeted Elizabeth outside the thick, bubbly glass of her bedroom window. Sunlight cut through the clear air and sparked off the grass and trees. As she peered out, she shivered and bounced from one foot to the other to avoid contact with the cold floor. She could see her breath in the chilly room. Ice crystals traced the edges of the water in the bowl on the washstand and she decided to wait to wash her face. The braided rug on the floor offered a little respite for chilly feet. Dressing quickly, she donned an everyday dress of light wool the color of buckskin with a white batiste collar. Then she flung the quilt over her bed and dashed downstairs as speedily as her voluminous frock would allow.

An aspect of life in 1850, the privy, or, as Aunt Ruth referred to it, "the necessary," was one to which she didn't think she would ever become accustomed. She had moments of true fear at the lack of sanitation. The deficiency of personal hygiene among those of every walk of life resulted in some powerful odors. The fact that she smelled as bad as everyone else left her yearning for a hot shower. Even more alluring was a long soak in a delicious tub of electrically heated water instead of lukewarm Saturday night ablutions that took place while she crouched in a round wooden tub in the kitchen. For privacy, Rachel held up a quilt and looked the other way.

Elizabeth gathered her courage along with her skirts and dashed through the yard scattering chickens on the way. Fortunately the cooler weather had allowed the noxious fumes from the outhouse to dissipate somewhat. She scurried back to the warmth of the kitchen.

After breakfast, Rachel washed dishes while Elizabeth dried. Aunt Ruth rocked contently in her chair in the corner, piecing fabric scraps for a quilt top.

"I'll get that bread dough on to rise in a little bit. I'd like to get some baking done today. How about a pumpkin pie for supper? I need to use up some of those eggs and that extra cream. Rachel? Do you want to churn this morning?"

"I can spell you, Rachel, that way it will go much faster." Elizabeth volunteered.

There was scuffling on the porch. Elizabeth opened the door to find Alice Ayres struggling with a bundle of tattered, bloodstained and growling rags.

"Hello, Mrs. Scott. I was wondering…if, perhaps, maybe you could help me?"

"Well, Alice, come in, please. What can I do for you?"

A muffled howl erupted from the swaddled lump.

Rachel looked at Elizabeth, alarmed.

"Oh, it's not *me* actually, it's this poor little cat!" The youngster folded back a corner of the wrapping to reveal a very dirty, very sick-looking cat. It growled weakly in fear and pain. "I found her in the carriage house this morning. She has a cut leg. It's very bad and starting to mortify."

Elizabeth settled onto the kitchen floor and drew the animal onto her aproned lap. Alice sat beside her.

"You see," she explained, "Father is out in the country on a call and Mother has no idea when he will be back. Rachel, I mean, Miss White, told me that you used to do a lot of doctoring with your husband, and I just thought…" Her voice trailed off and the freckles on her face stood out as her face paled. "I'm sorry."

"Don't you worry about talking about Dr. Scott, Alice. It's nice to hear his name spoken aloud," Elizabeth broke in briskly. "Now, let's see what we can do for this little critter."

Ignoring the cat's protests, she gently removed the makeshift bandage from the wounded front leg and was taken aback at the severity of the injury. The five-inch gash was to the bone and the skin flap hung down over its paw. Blood oozed steadily from the cut. By the looks of the amount of blood dried in the animal's drab brown and gold fur and the paleness of its gums, it had lost quite a bit. As she continued her evaluation of the animal's condition, she noted its ribs jutting from beneath the filthy, matted coat. The cat's green eyes were dull with shock. It didn't look good, but she didn't want to let on to Alice who looked on with an expression of bright expectation.

Caleb came into the kitchen and peered over Elizabeth's shoulder and grimaced.

"Better be careful there, Belle. That looks like one of those wild cats that hang around town. Something musta got a holt of her. Looks like she's pretty well used up. Maybe I ought to put it out of its misery."

Alice's eyes widened with alarm and Rachel glared at Caleb over the top of the girl's head.

"But…" He said, fumbling, his eyes on Rachel. "She just might…uh…pull through–with Dr. Belle on the job," he finished heartily. "Uh, guess I'll go help Pa mend harness."

Rachel nodded approvingly at her struggling fiancé. "Poor creature, she's not much more than a kitten!" she cooed, as Caleb beat a hasty retreat out to the barn.

"I'll get you some clean rags and soft soap, Elizabeth," offered Aunt Ruth.

"Thank-you," Elizabeth said, continuing her assessment. "Rachel, could you get me a basin of warm water with a small handful of salt dissolved in it? And, Aunt Ruth, could I have a pair of scissors, a razor and your very finest needle and thread? I promise I will clean everything up as good as new and buy you a new pack of needles."

"Why, yes, child, and I can certainly spare a needle!" Aunt Ruth hurried out of the room.

"Let's take her out on the porch where the light is better." Elizabeth suggested, gingerly trying to get up without disturbing the cat. It merely closed its eyes and sighed softly, as all its fight dissolved.

Alice rushed to open the door and Elizabeth carried the cat out to a worktable on the porch, leaving a trail of blood droplets across the floor. The little tabby did not have much time left.

Elizabeth gently cleaned the wound, shaving the fur from

around it while Rachel changed the water as it reddened. Then Elizabeth trimmed the ragged edges of the wound and, using Aunt Ruth's sewing supplies, took ten sutures. The cat only reacted once, but Alice held its head down, murmuring softly, and it immediately quieted. The leg was wrapped in clean rags and the sick animal laid in a crate lined with wheat straw. The box was put in a warm spot by the fire.

Elizabeth stood up and gingerly eased the kinks out of her back. "There we go, Alice. Aunt Ruth and Rachel will attest to the fact that I'm not much of a seamstress, so these stitches are a little lumpy, but I think they'll do. Let's let her rest for a while, and then your work begins."

"Whatever I need to do," the little girl declared with determination as she flipped her auburn braids over her shoulder and pushed up her sleeves, ready for duty, "I'll do it!"

"She's lost a lot of blood and needs to replace the fluids in her body. You'll need to get a few drops into her every few minutes," Elizabeth explained. Then in a gentler tone said, "You realize, don't you, that she's very seriously ill and may not live?"

"Oh, I can do that, I know I can!" Alice declared fervently. "And she will live!"

"Aunt Ruth could we have a little bit of broth? I'll thin it down with water and we'll add a tiny bit of salt and a drop of sweetening. Molasses or syrup will do."

Alice settled herself by the fire and stayed there the rest of the morning, urging the kitten to take a few drops now and then.

At noon Elizabeth offered to walk Alice home in order to introduce herself to Alice's mother. She also wanted to explain about the cat. Rachel promised to care for the tiny patient while they were gone.

As Elizabeth and Alice headed toward Junction, Ruth stood in the doorway watching them depart. Slowly shaking her head, she wondered aloud. "For someone who couldn't hem a handkerchief, she sure can stitch up a wound. Doctor Ayres ought to take the "Cincinnati Belle" on as a partner."

****

Elizabeth looked down at Alice as they walked along. She was a rather serious little girl. "You are very good with animals," she said.

The part in Alice's tightly plaited hair turned pink at the compliment. "Thank you. I like to take care of people, too, especially babies." She slipped her hand into Elizabeth's. "Mrs. Scott?"

"Please call me Elizabeth."

"Um, Elizabeth?"

"Yes?"

"I think I know what I want to name the cat."

Please don't let it be Elizabeth, she thought.

"And what is that," she asked aloud.

"Patience."

Elizabeth laughed at her own vanity and said to Alice, "Patience is perfect!"

CHAPTER 12

Rachel snipped a thread. "There," she said quietly. "It's finished." The dress lay across her lap. The genteel young woman smoothed out the folds and spread the full skirt around her. "What do you think?"

"Oh, Rachel!" Elizabeth caught her breath. "It's lovely. It really is. You're going to be beautiful." She stood back and admired the result of Rachel's painstaking work. Fifteen yards of embroidered satin billowed like a flower-sprigged cloud. Her eyes sparkled with the same blue of the tiny forget-me-nots and her flushed cheeks picked up the pink of the rosebuds.

Aunt Ruth hastened into the room, wiping her hands on a dishcloth. "Rachel, I think we…" She stopped short when she saw the completed gown. "Oh Rachel!" Then, as if the wedding hadn't already been the hub their lives had circled around for weeks, she squeaked and collapsed in a chair. "My land! The wedding is next week!" The flustered woman fanned herself with the cloth.

Elizabeth struggled to keep a straight face. She glanced at Rachel and saw that she was having the same problem.

Ruth was ticking items off on her fingers while talking to no one in particular. "Let's see now, I have to do the baking, although the ladies from the church are going to bring some pies. Then there's the cleaning. I can't do that until the very last…Rachel! What day is your family to arrive? No, never mind, I know…" Not waiting for an answer, she rushed on. "I have to check to make sure the inn is ready for them, and then I think we need to do a little decorating…" Her one-sided conversation became a mumble as she sank deep into thought.

Elizabeth and Rachel stared at the woman and laughed in unison, which brought Ruth out of her fluster. Realizing the picture she made, she joined in.

"I believe you two thought I took leave of my senses there

for a moment, didn't you?"

"Oh, Mother Ruth, I am so sorry!" Rachel apologized. "How could I be so rude?"

"Because I must make quite a sight, that's why!" Ruth laughed at herself.

"Aunt Ruth, could I do the decorating? I think I could come up with some good ideas," Elizabeth ventured.

"Why of course! That is, if it's all right with Rachel."

Rachel looked pleased. "I would be honored, Elizabeth. I'm certain that anything you create will be lovely!"

Elizabeth felt confident in her abilities to employ the bounty of autumn's harvest in decorating for the wedding. It was a relief to know that at last she would be making a worthy contribution to the wedding preparations. She would need Uncle William and his team and wagon. Perhaps she could also enlist Alice and the O'Dillon girls to help.

****

Later that afternoon, Elizabeth walked to Junction to get permission from the girls' mothers to help her collect items from the woods and fields. Because the wedding was a special occasion, all three were freed from their after school duties to help. Alice, Mary and Katherine were the envy of their female classmates. It was an honor to help with the beloved Miss White's wedding. The trio found it a difficult task to not swagger with self-importance.

Uncle William hitched up a small wagon lined with fresh straw for Elizabeth and her helpers. They loaded the bed of the wagon with pumpkins, cornshocks, dried grasses and wild grapevine and bittersweet from down along the riverbank.

Tired and dusty, the gathering crew headed home through the cooling dusk. The girls sat at the open end of the wagon, swinging their feet over the edge, munching the crisp, red apples that William provided. Mary began humming and Katherine joined in, singing a song in a language unfamiliar to Elizabeth.

Knowing that the girls' parents came over from Ireland, she thought perhaps it was Gaelic, possibly a lullaby they learned at their mother's knee.

*****

The shipping year was drawing to a close as November approached. The wedding date had been planned so that the White family would have ample time for visiting and for return travel before the end of the canal season. Rachel's mother, father and youngest brother, Ezekial were expected to arrive from Cleveland a week before the wedding. However, as the day drew nearer, there was no sign or word from her family.

Though she strove to keep her fears in check, Rachel was becoming alarmed. Although the Ohio canal system had eased some of the discomfort of travel, it was still a long, arduous and sometimes unpredictable trip. The Whites would first have to take a ship from Cleveland across Lake Erie to the port at Toledo and from there embark on a canal packet.

Her mind frantically explored all the disastrous possibilities that might have befallen her loved ones. Maybe they had met with illness or misfortune along the way. Unsavory characters preyed on travelers. Rachel, always sensitive to the feelings of others and not wanting to be an emotional burden on the Hudsons, hid her fears. Her endeavors did not go unnoticed by Elizabeth, who heard her sobbing in her room at night. Finally, as the day before the wedding dawned without sign or word of her family, her mask of bravery slipped.

CHAPTER 13

The autumn of 1850 had been calm. Foggy mornings dissolved into warm, golden afternoons and opal twilights. The day before the wedding began with an angry red sky that quickly gave way to threatening clouds. In the afternoon, dry leaves, blown by the wind, raced and skittered across open ground and piled into drifts against the brick house. The leaves still clinging to branches rattled and spun in crazy circles. Each gust of wind brought more clouds that muddied the sky into an early dusk.

At dinner that evening, the Hudsons, made uneasy by the threatening weather and worried about the fate of Rachel's family, ate quietly and without appetite. The only sound was the occasional clink of utensil against plate and the crackle of fire on the hearth. The room glowed in the lamplight. Curtains at the windows stood out crisp and snowy with starch. Anything that required polishing had been buffed to a shine at least twice. Rugs had been taken up in anticipation of dancing. Borrowed chairs and benches lined the walls in the parlor, ready for guests. Elizabeth's decorations, arranged in corners and on tabletops, lent the warmth of muted harvest color.

William, in an attempt to break the crushing silence, cleared his throat. "Place looks real nice, Ruth."

"Thank you Pa. I couldn't have done it without the girls. And Elizabeth did such a wonderful job, didn't she?" she replied to the compliment. Turning to Rachel, she said, "Honey, can't you take a little something? You need to keep your strength up."

Rachel's wordlessly shook her head as tears pooled in her eyes.

Caleb, normally a competent young man with a ready smile, was reduced to helplessly patting Rachel's tightly clasped hands. An evening that should have been overflowing with joy and anticipation had the air of a deathwatch.

"Please excuse me, I think I'll retire now," Rachel whispered. She turned and her footsteps could be heard as she ran up her room.

Caleb turned sad eyes to Elizabeth. "Will you go to her? No need to say anything, just be with her." He stumbled over his words.

As Elizabeth followed Rachel up the steep steps, the rain came, hitting the house with great force. Upstairs water drummed on the roof and streamed in a solid sheet down the window glass. Holding her candle higher, Elizabeth found Rachel face down and motionless across her bed. Quietly she lowered herself to the floor beside the bed and gently placed her hand on the grief-stricken young woman's arm. Just as the storm had finally broken, so did Rachel's shell of strength. Her shoulders quaked, the quilt only partially muffled her sobs.

"This isn't about the wedding!" she choked. "I just want them to be well and out of harm's way!"

"They probably are," Elizabeth said soothingly while smoothing Rachel's hair from her wet face. "So many times we worry ourselves sick over someone we love and then it all turns out fine." Suddenly a memory from her modern life broke through and she saw herself sitting by her dying husband's side. Her heart lurched. Abruptly as it came, the feeling was gone. She got up and rummaged through a drawer for a handkerchief.

"Do you think so?" Rachel sat up. For the first time in days, hope glimmered in her eyes. "I am so anxious to see them, especially Mother. I do miss her so. The Hudsons have truly become family to me, and this is as it should be, but I want to see my lovely Mother! I need to know that she, Father and Ezekial are…" She used Elizabeth's word. "Okay." Then wiped her eyes with the handkerchief that was offered.

Downstairs, the rest of the family tried to decide what was to be done about the wedding.

Caleb spoke, his usually smooth brow was creased. "Pa, the circuit preacher is going to be here just this Sunday. You know he only comes around once a month. I hate to hold off our wedding because Ma and the girls have worked so hard and everything is ready." He paused.

"But I want to do what is right and fitting." He wrapped his big callused hands around an ironstone mug of tea, trying to warm them. The pounding rain had caused a damp chill to seep through the bricks. "It is important to Rachel and to me, that her family be here.

His father nodded thoughtfully, puffing on a small clay pipe. Light from the fire glinted off the silver in his thick beard."Son, it can't be helped. All the cooking and baking can be done again. It won't go to waste. You need to leave it up to Rachel. Let her decide. If she makes the decision, it will easier for her to live with, I believe."

Ruth refilled the cups. "Caleb, you'll both want to hold happy memories of the day in your hearts, not of sadness and grief."

Rachel followed Elizabeth into the room. Although her face was blotchy from crying, she was dry-eyed.

She squared her shoulders and took a deep breath. "I've given this a great deal of thought and if Caleb and everyone agrees. If you all think it's proper, that is..." She took a deep breath and smiled shakily. "We should go on with the ceremony. My parents would want us to..." Her voice quavered, "No matter what."

William was a quiet man and considered his words carefully before he voiced his opinions. He sat silently for a moment considering the situation and then said in his deep voice, "Rachel, I believe you have a made a wise decision." He turned to include Caleb. "There will be many times during your life together as man and wife when you both will have to make difficult choices. As partners and as parents, if you are so blessed, you will be made stronger by these trials. You will gain spiritual strength *if* you choose to learn from them. You will find that words spoken by that circuit preacher tomorrow are just that, words. You two have the responsibility of making those words mean something." He got up and took Caleb's left hand and Rachel's right and held them together in his own commodious grasp. "Welcome to the family, daughter, we're proud to claim you."

The couple hugged, Aunt Ruth dabbed at her eyes with a corner of her apron and Elizabeth swallowed hard.

****

Later, Elizabeth lay in bed and listened to the storm raging. Tree limbs thrashed and creaked in the gale and the deluge continued. Thunder grumbled and cracked and lightening repeatedly lit the room, flashing so brightly it left negative images when she closed her eyes. Leaves and twigs dashed against the window, hung for moment then were whisked off into the night by the wind. She pitied any human or animal that might be out in such weather. Even so, Caleb had braved the elements and returned to his farm to tend to the stock and make sure the little cabin was as clean as Rachel and Elizabeth left it the day before.

The rest of the household had retired, too. Rachel had been unable to rest for the past three nights, fretting about her family. Finally, exhausted, she had fallen into a deep sleep.

As Elizabeth lay watching the rain sheet the glass and lightening spear the sky, her thoughts wandered to Mitch. Since she had come here, the world she left had been only a cloudy memory. Why had Mitch's death flooded back so vividly and ebbed away just as quickly? But she *had* felt a swift stab of pain in her heart. It was peculiar. She remembered her life from before much like she would recall a favorite book or film, but it didn't feel particularly *real.* The details were there, yet the faces were slightly out of focus and her emotions clouded. She wasn't homesick, or at all concerned about getting back, she realized. It seemed odd that she possessed no desire to return to her family, friends and career. This revelation did not frighten or excite her and she accepted it without question. Despite the thunder that pounded relentlessly, over and over, Elizabeth was lulled by the steady beat of rain on the slate roof and fell into a restful slumber.

****

Elizabeth jerked awake. Disoriented, she struggled out of a deep, dreamless sleep. Over the din of wind and rain slamming against the house came the clamor of church bells. The hammering, which she decided was coming from downstairs, began again.

Male voices, deepened by alarm, shouted. "Hudson! Hudson! Wake up, man!"

CHAPTER FOURTEEN

Elizabeth vaulted out of bed and hurried to the top of the stairs just as Uncle William yanked open the back door. Aunt Ruth huddled behind him, her wrapper clutched at her throat with one hand, a candle held aloft in the other. The draft from outside caused the candle flame to jump and flicker, making eerie shadows leap weirdly from floor to ceiling to wall. Elizabeth ran down the steps and into the kitchen.

On the porch were two men, mud-covered, soaking wet and carrying shovels. Elizabeth did not recognize the spokesman, but her heart gave a leap when the other man, bearing a torch, stepped forward. Even though she had only just met and spent one brief afternoon with him, in the sputtering light of the torch, she immediately recognized the dark, luminous eyes of Daniel Mahafy.

"The canal! She's goin' ta wash out at the aqueduct!" shouted the first man.

Daniel spoke up. He was all business, a captain used to giving orders. His flirtatious manner of their afternoon stroll, only one short week ago, had been erased in the face of an emergency on the canal, his canal.

"Mr. Hudson, get Caleb, too! We need all the men we can get! I can't ever remember an October storm like this!" He nodded politely at Ruth. "Mrs. Hudson." He looked intently at Elizabeth for a brief moment. "Mrs. Scott." Then he was gone into the turbulent night.

Uncle William ran to dress while Aunt Ruth scurried about gathering his warmest coat and heavy boots. He hurried out the door, flinging his coat on as he went. "I'll fetch Caleb. He could have heard the church bell, if the wind didn't drown it out, and is already headed this way. Don't know when we'll be back!"

With shaking hands, Elizabeth lit the lamp on the table. She shivered with cold and excitement. The aqueduct, a stone, bridge-like structure that carried the canal over Five-mile Creek, if it washed out, could send the waters of the canal flooding into Junction.

"I'll make coffee and take it to the mill!" Aunt Ruth shouted out the door after Uncle William. "Be careful!" Her candle flame fluttered and went out as she slammed the door against the blast of wind and rain.

The bottom step creaked. Ruth and Elizabeth turned simultaneously. Rachel, pale and ghostly in a long, white nightgown, stood at the bottom of the stairs, clinging to the banister. Her shining, sable hair, usually carefully braided every night, tumbled over her shoulders and down her back. She swayed wearily.

"Mother?" she whispered hopefully, peering at the door.

Ruth shook her head sadly. "No, child, it's the canal. The storm has washed out the banks by the aqueduct. They need every able body to repair it."

Rachel sagged. "Well, you'll be needing help," she said flatly. "I'll go dress."

Ruth stopped her by placing her work-knotted hands on the young woman's shoulders. "Rachel," she said gently, "You will do no such thing. It's your weddin' day and no bride under my roof is goin' to do a lick of work on her special day!"

Then she turned the exhausted young woman around and with mock severity said, "Go back to bed! You need your sleep. I know you haven't been sleeping much the past week." She tempered her gruffness with a smile. "I've Elizabeth here to help me."

Rachel quietly returned to her room.

Aunt Ruth went to dress while Elizabeth tied an apron on over her nightgown and started water boiling for coffee.

Aunt Ruth called from the bedroom. "Elizabeth, start slicing that bread and spread it thick with butter."

"Aunt Ruth, isn't that supposed to be for the wedding supper?" Elizabeth protested.

"Those men will be near-starved when they finally get a chance to eat, she said as she re-entered the room, while coiling her long, gray-streaked braid onto the back of her head.

"We'll take everything to the mill. That's where everyone will gather once the situation is under control."

"I was just thinking of how hard you worked kneading and baking all that bread," she said, sawing a loaf.

After a second of silence, "Is it really dangerous?" Elizabeth questioned her aunt.

"It can be. It's dark and the water level is way up over the banks," she said, gathering some biscuits left from supper into a basket. "There can be cave-ins or mud-slides as the water washes over. The most dangerous part is the horses and mules, trampling around all panicky-like. You just never know what's going to happen. Some people call the Miami and Erie "The Irish Graveyard."

"The Irish Graveyard?" Elizabeth asked. "Why?"

"They say there's a dead Irish man for every mile of the canal."

"That's horrible!" Elizabeth suppressed a shudder. "All from accidents?"

"Well, there were plenty of mishaps during construction, but I figure most of the deaths were from bad food, too much whiskey and the fever." Ruth said, carefully removing layers of gauzy cloth from a wheel of her legendary cheese.

Elizabeth's nursing instinct was aroused. "What kind of fever?"

"No one is quite sure what caused it," Ruth said. "Could have been the bad night air comin' from the swamps. Lots o' folks didn't have window glass, still don't, just greased brown paper, if that. It's hard to tell what all got in." Her brisk voice trailed off as she remembered. "It was an unpredictable thing, first you'd shiver and shake, felt like you'd never be warm again. Then the fever'd come. It'd go higher and higher…" She paused and took a deep breath. "The peculiar thing was that a body would seem to get well and then, it would come back all of a sudden without warning. Fever n' ague it's called."

Elizabeth immediately recognized the disease her aunt

described as malaria. "You know…before…uh, Dr. Scott died, he was doing some research, some studies - about fever. He suspected mosquitoes," she said knowing that she was rewriting history a bit.

"Mosquitoes! My land!" Ruth exclaimed. "To think such a little thing could cause such a was a terrible time, though the good Lord knows there are enough of them. Whole families practically starved to death because no one had the strength to go out and work." She paused, deep in thought, staring down at her hands. "Then there was the typhoid…It was a terrible, sad time."

The woman bowed her head and her busy hands stilled.

"Aunt Ruth?" Elizabeth peered at her aunt through the dim light. "Are you all right?"

The older woman started and looked up at Elizabeth, her merry eyes veiled by sadness. "You see, Elizabeth, this big, fine house was filled to the rafters with laughter and life.

William and I lost three of our dear children to the typhoid fever. I don't know how Caleb survived. He was a baby. We thought for a while we were goin' to lose him, too, but he pulled through." She sighed, weighted with the grief she was revisiting. "There was Joseph, he was six and a finer boy there never was. And the twins…Libby, actually Elizabeth, just like you, and Lucas, they were four. My babies never had a chance."

"Oh, Aunt Ruth, I didn't know! I…don't know what to say." Elizabeth wiped the tears from her cheeks.

"Well," the woman squared her shoulders resolutely and began slapping slices of the cheese between the pieces of bread, "we didn't suffer any more than most of the families in these parts. As for you not knowing about it…I suppose people just don't talk much about such things. Brings back too many memories. Although," she paused, "it would have been a great comfort to be able to sit and remember the children with someone. William, oh, he was tormented, he thought he should have done more. Though, I swear I don't know what more he could have done. He never slept a wink, not once from the time Joseph first took sick…and then Lucas. We didn't even have time to bury

Joseph until the other two was took."

"Oh, Aunt Ruth," Elizabeth clasped her hand tightly. "How did you do it, how did you get through it?"

"Child, I truly do not know. That first year of mourning, we fed the stock and did what needed to be done, but it was hard to know why we didn't just sit and let ourselves go, too."

She sighed and shook her head. "The good Lord, He knows. He answers all prayers, just not always with the answers we want to hear. We still had Caleb and now Rachel has come into our lives and hopefully, well…" She shrugged her shoulders a little sheepishly and her cheeks reddened slightly.

I don't mean to be disrespectful, but where are they, Joseph, Libby and Lucas, buried?"

"Oh, over in that little grove of maple trees by the lane to Caleb's. I go to visit sometimes, when I feel the need."

"I'm glad you told me, I feel more a part of the family. I would be honored if you would take me there sometime, Aunt Ruth."

"Oh honey, you are a part of this family! I don't know if it's because your name is the same as our baby girl, but I took to you the minute I laid eyes on you." Ruth squeezed Elizabeth's hand back. "I would be happy to take you and tell you about our babies," Ruth's voice, usually strong and purposeful, quavered.

She shook herself to shed the cloak of sadness that shadowed the room. "Now then," Ruth straightened, giving the impression that she was physically pushing back the air of sadness that had crept into the room, "this is a day of celebration. And wild as it is, this is the day that the Lord hath made."

The heavy tread of booted feet sounded on the back porch and the door burst open, aided by the blustering wind. Caleb stuck his head in. "Ma? Pa said for me stop here and get the grub and take it to the mill so's you wouldn't have to go out in this storm. No sense in my ma and Belle gettin' all wet!" He left with a shovel over his shoulder and carrying a food-laden basket in one hand and swinging a large coffeepot from the other.

Aunt Ruth pushed the door shut against the stinging rain.

The downpour showed no sign of abating. She wiped her hands on her apron. "Well, Mrs. Scott, we have quite a day ahead of us and we need to get what rest we can. Your Uncle William and Cousin Caleb are sensible sorts. I think they will be all right. Besides, Caleb isn't going to take any unnecessary chances on his wedding day. So, back to bed with you. Shoo!"

Elizabeth was quite happy to slip her icy feet beneath the covers. She needed a few moments to still her mind as it raced about with the night's events: the storm, the washout, Rachel's missing family, Aunt Ruth's revelation about their children, the approaching wedding and…Daniel Mahafy. She would see him again within hours, at the wedding. She was flustered by her reaction to someone she barely knew. There was definitely something special about Daniel Mahafy, captain of the Wabash Queene.

CHAPTER 15

Elizabeth opened her eyes as dawn washed the room in pearly gray. The first thing she noticed was the absence of sound: the wind and rain no longer hammered against the brick house. The murmur of voices drifted up the stairs. Flipping the quilt back, Elizabeth grabbed her wrapper, as Aunt Ruth called it, and slipped it on over nightgown as she hurried to the banister. On her way she peeked into the other room and saw that Rachel was still asleep. Her shining hair lay tangled over the pillow. Even in her sleep she looked sad and pale. Elizabeth tiptoed down the stairs.

Three strangers, two men and a woman, were standing in the kitchen. They looked rumpled, weary and wet. The woman's hair straggled from beneath a drooping bonnet. When she smiled, her blue eyes sparkled just like Rachel's and there was no doubt as to their identity.

Aunt Ruth beamed at Elizabeth. "They are here and they are safe! Mr. and Mrs. White, Eziekial, I would like you to meet our niece, Elizabeth Hudson-Scott."

"Rachel will be thrilled when she sees you!" Elizabeth exclaimed.

"We are pleased to make your acquaintance, Mrs. Scott." Even in his bedraggled state, Mr. Boaz White exuded an air of sophistication.

Rachel's mother pressed her cold cheek to Elizabeth's in a damp hug. "I know I'm all wet, but we've so looked forward to meeting you, Elizabeth! I may call you Elizabeth, mightn't I?"

"Yes, yes, of course, please don't stand on ceremony!"

"I feel as if I know you already from Rachel's letters. You have been just like a sister to her. We had so many concerns about her decision to venture out, so far from her home. A proper young lady on her own, so used to the comforts of civilization, well, you know it just is not done in most circles. However, a group of young ladies from the academy was traveling west, well chaperoned, of course. And you know Rachel, so quiet in her ways, yet she insisted there was such a need for teachers and schools and such, out here in the wilderness and that she must come."

"Well, I don't know how much help I've been," Elizabeth protested. "I feel that I'm the one that has benefited from Rachel's friendship. I've always wanted a sister."

Ruth laughed. "Always wanted a sister! What do you call Hortense, Dorcas and Rebecca, if they aren't your older sisters?"

Elizabeth's face flamed as she stuttered a reply. "Well, I - I meant a *younger* sister, of course," as the words left her mouth, she rapidly sent up a fervent silent prayer, that Elizabeth Hudson-Scott, late of Cincinnati, Ohio, was youngest in her family.

No contradiction followed her statement and Elizabeth fired off a thank you as quickly and in the same direction as her plea for mercy.

Mrs. White removed her sodden velvet bonnet. "What a journey! We thought we would never get here! Because of the washout, we had to travel the last few miles in a farm wagon!"

"I believe my dear Emaline thrives on adventure!" Boaz White smiled fondly at his wife as he helped her remove her dripping woolen cloak.

"I fear that I am solely responsible for the distress we have caused you all." Ezekial limped forward and ruefully held up a cane.

"Mr. White sent word, but obviously it never arrived," Mrs. White said.

Rachel's father explained. "Ezekial, here, decided that the ship's captain and crew needed his assistance while we were under sail to Toledo. He slipped and injured his ankle. For a while we were anxious, fearing serious injury, as he could not walk upon it."

He patted the shoulder of his son's waterlogged, yet still elegant cape. "However, we finally procured the services of a physician, who assured us that it was merely a bad sprain. We were relieved there were no broken bones. After a week, the swelling was greatly reduced. The doctor bandaged it so that Ezekial could hobble about, then sent us on our way west."

"It was my impetuous foolishness, thinking that the lads were in need of *my* assistance!" Ezekial apologized. "I must confess that I allowed myself to succumb to a common boyhood fantasy of experiencing life on the high seas." He laughed heartily at himself. "As you can see, although I am loathe to admit it, my present occupation as captain of desk and chair suits me far better than one of adventure!"

"Well, perhaps. However, you cannot take personal responsibility for yesterday's tempest!" his father assured him.

Elizabeth built up the fire in the parlor and spread the guests' wet wraps near it to dry.

"How is Rachel?" Mrs. White asked.

"Why don't you go on up and waken her." Ruth suggested. "I can't think of a better gift for a bride, can you Elizabeth?" Ruth lowered her voice slightly. "I must admit, I was fairly worried about her, she being so upset and all. She was simply exhausted wondering what could have become of you, poor lamb."

****

William and Caleb returned shortly after that, tired and muddy, but happy, as the canal had been saved. Aunt Ruth and Elizabeth got a quick, hot breakfast together and both families sat down to share the repast with healthy appetites. Afterward, Uncle William took the Whites to the inn then came home to catch up on some sleep. Caleb went home to rest and prepare for the wedding.

Elizabeth and Ruth fairly flew around the house readying for the evening ceremony. When Elizabeth stepped outside the air was clear and cold. The wind had stripped the last of the leaves from the trees and plastered them to the house and out buildings. Branches littered the ground and puddles stood everywhere, reflecting a sky washed clean of clouds.

Elizabeth dropped an armload of broken branches near the woodpile and turned to see three small figures picking their way around the puddles on the path to the brick house. It was Alice, Mary and Katherine coming to help with last minute preparations for the wedding. Seeing Elizabeth, they waved and soon were on seated on the porch and removing muddy boots.

"Oh my, that was a storm last night!" Alice exclaimed. "I brought Patience into my room because I just knew she would be frightened of the thunder. Ma would skin me if she knew I let her sleep on my pillow," she confessed.

Mary looked soberly at Elizabeth. "Mrs. Scott, we have practiced and practiced, but still, I'm afraid."

"What's to be afeared of, Mary?" Katherine asked. "We sing at home all the time with Pa when he plays his fiddle. We sing for Sunday school and you never get scared."

"I don't know, this just seems so…so…*important*."

"It is important, Mary, but only because Rachel is so fond of you two. She never had any little sisters, but when she came to Junction, here you all were, just like you were waiting for her.

The three looked at each other, beaming.

"That's why it means so much to her that you'll be singing for a very special time in her life. She doesn't expect a perfect performance," Elizabeth assured. "Besides, you could croak like a frog and it wouldn't make a whit of difference to Rachel and Caleb! To them it would still sound beautiful." Elizabeth dusted her hands together. "I know something else! If we don't get busy, we won't be ready!"

The girls were arranging the borrowed chairs and benches into rows, chattering happily among themselves, when Rachel came down from her room where her parents were preparing to rest, and welcomed them. "There are my two songbirds!"

"Hello, Miss White! We're so excited! I know I won't forget this day as long as I live!" Katherine exclaimed.

"Miss White! Guess who came into town during that storm?" Alice asked, dimpling.

"I do know my parents and brother Ezekial came in through

that terrible storm last night."

"That's not the only terrible thing that came into town last night…" Katherine giggled.

"Katherine," her older sister warned, "let Alice tell it, it's her story."

"Well," Alice paused dramatically, "Father was waiting at the Fordyce's mill in case there were any injuries. And he said that a wagonload of folks that were forced off the canal 'cause of the storm drove up. He said you could hear moanin' and cryin' while the wagon was clear off up the street. He said it sounded so bad, he was almost afraid to look in the wagon for fear of what he might see." She giggled, picturing her stern father, who always struck her as fearless, holding his hands over his eyes. "You'll never guess who it was…"

Rachel clapped her hands together. "I know! Portia! Portia Fordyce!"

Peals of laughter erupted simultaneously from all three girls.

Katherine minced around on her toes with her nose in the air. "Mary! *Do* be a dear and wipe my boots!" She pretended to rap her sister with a fan. "They are *simply* ghastly!"

"Katherine! Don't you forget that Portia's father employs Pa and that's what puts food on our table." Mary admonished. "She is a sight to see, though," she admitted to Elizabeth with a wide smile.

"I imagine that she and her mother came back just for the wedding," Rachel said. "Elizabeth, you will be introduced some of, no, the finest citizens of Junction tonight." She smiled impishly and raised her eyebrows at the girls who looked at Elizabeth expectantly.

"I can hardly wait!" Elizabeth declared.

Alice, Mary and Katherine giggled.

CHAPTER 16

An archway of wild grapevine decked with bittersweet and crimson oak leaves welcomed the wedding guests to the brick house. Golden corn shocks, colorful pumpkins and squash lined the porches and flanked the fireplace in the parlor. Elizabeth had fashioned grapevine and bittersweet into a garland that festooned the banister that William had carved by hand when the house was built.

People arrived early, with hampers full of food. William, Caleb and Boaz White stood together greeting guests as they entered. The young circuit preacher hailed the arriving townsfolk heartily. He was slightly nervous since he was new to the territory and had never performed nuptials in front of such a gathering. Ezekial was arranged in a settee with his sprained ankle elevated. Aunt Ruth fussed around him like an old hen. First, draping a shawl over his shoulders to ward off drafts, which, with the crush of bodies in the room, had very little chance of occurring, then positioning cushions here and there.

Elizabeth, an apron over her apricot silk taffeta gown, took in the all the sights and sounds of Junction's social event of the decade when she wasn't shuttling between the kitchen and the two parlors. Her skirts rustled with every step of her matching slippers. Rachel had, with her usual thoughtfulness, taken time to arrange Elizabeth's unruly hair. It fell in ringlets over her ears, with a small knot in back, surrounded by tiny satin rosebuds that Elizabeth had found in her capacious trunk.

Rachel's students, along with their parents and siblings were in attendance. The O'Dillons came in with Charlie, the little brother "who stuck like a burr." In spite of an angelic crown of blond curls, he was full of "spit and vinegar," according to Uncle William. Living up to that appraisal, within a few minutes of his arrival, the boy had managed to swipe a handful of bittersweet berries and was pelting his classmates with them. With a large, well-muscled hand, Mr. O'Dillon promptly put a stop to the shenanigans with a simple squeeze to his son's shoulder. Mary, Katherine and Alice were waiting upstairs with Rachel and her mother.

Alice's parents, Dr. and Mrs. Ayres, who had come early with Alice, sat beside the Cunninghams. Mrs. Cunningham, resplendent in her best dress, smiled across the room at Elizabeth. Just then, the steady murmuring in the room, much like the hum around a beehive, stilled at the sound of a carriage drawing up outside the house.

Caleb, elegant in his frock coat, grinned at Elizabeth and twitched his head slightly in the direction of the door. A young woman entered the room with great flair. Dressed in satin to rival any wedding gown, she was petite and peeped quite prettily out from under her wide-brimmed bonnet. Her flaxen hair cascaded in ringlets about her heart-shaped face, but her smile, that revealed small, even teeth, was brittle. Behind her was a dumpy little woman wearing an elaborate and obviously expensive, ensemble that only emphasized her squat physique. She entered on the arm of a tall, spare gentleman with a sour, pinched expression. With a great deal of fuss they finally settled into the back row of chairs.

That has to be Portia Fordyce, Elizabeth thought to herself. She quickly scanned the crowded room, knowing in her heart there was one person she especially hoped to see. But, she was disappointed. She returned to the kitchen to remove her apron and ascertain, for one last time, that all was ready for the wedding supper.

Daniel Mahafy leaned in the kitchen doorway, his tall frame nearly filling it. Elizabeth jumped and her hand flew to her throat. "Mr. Mahafy!"

His hat was in his hand and there was a grin on his face. This elegantly attired gentleman scarcely resembled the mud-spattered individual who had stood in that very door only hours earlier.

"Cap'n Daniel to you, Madam. Actually, Mrs. Scott, I prefer

Daniel. Formalities without just cause are a vexation to me."

"Daniel, then." Elizabeth extended her hand. "Come, sit with me. The ceremony is ready to start."

They slipped into the middle parlor and, as no empty chairs remained, joined the overflow of guests standing in the back of the room.

An elderly man proffered his seat to Elizabeth, but she demurred, stating that she would be needed shortly.

The young minister cleared his throat. To a crowd of onlookers that was already squeezed together in an almost improper manner, he announced, "All right, folks, let's us gather in."

There was a rise in the level of conversational noise and a scraping of seats, then the crowd quieted expectantly. Aunt Ruth went up to the fireplace to stand beside Uncle William and Caleb. She looked lovely in her new dress of finely spun wool, the color of a midnight sky. The evening's excitement brought a flush to her cheeks that erased the years.

Mr. White crossed the room and held out his hand to Mrs. White as she swept down into the room in a dress that was the height of fashion. There were so many rows of wide lace flounces circling the belled skirt it was difficult for her to navigate the stairs gracefully. There was a hushed murmur in reaction to her fine costume. He smiled at her with affection, patted her hand and then nodded at the three glowing faces that peeked through the railings.

Mary and Katherine stepped self-consciously down the stairs to the front of the room and turned around. Their father stood up, his worn fiddle at the ready. The sisters began to sing, their voices blending in harmony with the sweet music of the violin. Elizabeth was entranced as their self-consciousness fell away and their voices rose and filled the room. "*O Perfect Love, all human thought transcending...*" The sisters lifted their eyes upward and sang the words from their hearts, with no thought of the people present. They were one voice. In their ice blue dresses and silvery blond braids that wreathed, halo-like, around their heads, they were angelic. The hymn ended softly as the last note of the fiddle faded away.

Next, Alice, her hair put up for the occasion, came down holding a small handful of wildflowers that had managed to escape the storm. She stood beside Aunt Ruth, who put her hand on the girl's shoulder. Alice's face was lit with a beaming smile until she turned around to face the crowd. Then, suddenly embarrassed, she stared at the floor.

Caleb's face stilled and everyone in the room knew that Rachel had appeared at the top of the banister. Mr. White held his arm out for his daughter as she descended. Her shining, dark hair was caught up in a circlet of pink satin roses. Her gown, scattered with the tiny blossoms of forget-me-nots and roses, was simple in line. Full sleeves began off the shoulder and ended in a ruffle of lace, tied with tiny ribbons, at the elbow. The snug-fitting bodice had a long, pointed waist that gave way to yards and yards of skirt that pouffed out over many layers of petticoats. Rachel was smiling and calm. With her head held high, she swept through the room on her father's arm to where Caleb waited for her with his hand outstretched.

CHAPTER 17

"Blessed be the tie that binds our hearts in Christian love; the fellowship of human hearts is like to that above..." Mary and Katherine O'Dillon sang, their sweet, young faces glowing in the candlelight. The newly united couple, Mr. and Mrs. Caleb Hudson and their parents, made their way around the room welcoming their guests. Then the wedding supper began. People disappeared into the crowd gathered around the laden board and emerged with heaping plates. An even dozen of Aunt Ruth's plump cockerels had been sacrificed for the golden-crusted chicken pie that ran with rich yellow gravy. Friends and neighbors brought with them bubbling baked beans, breads and pickles of all kinds, sugared doughnuts, apple and pumpkin pies and cold apple cider fresh from the barrel in the springhouse.

As guests cleaned their heaping plates and staggered outside into the cool evening for fresh air, young men cleared the chairs from the parlor. Michael O'Dillon, Katherine and Mary's father, tuned his fiddle while friends and relatives adjusted their instruments, which included another fiddle, a small harp, several fifes and dulcimers. One musician cradled a large, flat drum, called a bodhran, vertically between his knees and hammered out a quick practice rhythm with a small mallet. It looked to Elizabeth much like a large tambourine without the cymbals. Those guests, whose religious beliefs forbade dancing and similar merriment, politely wished the new couple well and took their leave.

Soon foot-tapping music swelled to fill the room. Michael O'Dillon's thick, work-callused hands were nimble on the bow when it came to coaxing a tune from his fiddle, battered and scarred as it was from years of faithful service. Caleb, proud, and Rachel, flushed with excitement, led off, weaving in and out in a lively reel. Other partners danced merrily down the line, while those standing on the side clapped and stomped in time to the music.

Life was grueling on the Ohio frontier and times for celebrations few. Farmers, canalers and trades people, many of them immigrated from Ireland, Scotland and Germany, were drawn by the opportunities presented with the opening, only a few short years before, of the canals. Although the area was rapidly becoming settled, it was still a rugged existence and when there was cause for a frolic, the event was enjoyed by the entire family. As the brick house heated up, perspiring dancers stepped out to cool off in the brisk night air. Men stood around smoking pipes and admiring the horses and mules that carried many of the guests from surrounding farms to the party. Small boys romped in the barnyard, clambering over rigs.

Girls of all ages gathered in knots to giggle and dance in the corners. Young parents, remembering their own weddings, danced, carefree for the moment, while their babies slept in their grandparents' arms. Sleepy toddlers, faces sticky and smudged, nestled in piles of coats and dozed, oblivious to the noise.

Elizabeth watched, fascinated, as the dancers went through their paces. Her feet tapped and her skirts bounced in time to the music as she clapped along. Across the room she could see impish Katherine teasing Mary with a perfect imitation of Portia Fordyce, who had just swooped by on the arm of a smitten admirer. Alice had both hands to her mouth, while her shoulders shook with mirth.

Working her way around to the girls, Elizabeth crossed her arms and with mock indignation declared, "And just what are you three up to?"

Katherine started guiltily. "Elizabeth! I was just..." Her voiced dropped to a conspiratory whisper. "Did you see her? Isn't she a sight?"

"See whom, Katherine?" Elizabeth asked innocently, although it was quite obvious by the way the girls kept sneaking what they thought were furtive glances at the object of their mischief.

"There are so many guests here tonight, are you referring to a particular person?" she queried, her face devoid of curiosity.

"Miss Fordyce! Portia!" said Katherine in a stage whisper loud enough to prompt several guests on the edge of the dance floor to stop clapping and turn around.

"Sh-h-h-h!" Mary and Alice hissed simultaneously, clamping their hands over the younger girl's mouth.

Mary scanned the crowd, worried that their mother might have seen what Katherine was up to. It seemed no matter how hard she tried to explain that it was her younger sister's doing, she was held responsible. It was a heavy burden for a twelve-year-old girl to bear. Mary sighed with relief. Ma was sitting out in the kitchen. There was another baby on the way and she needed to rest often these days.

"You just better be careful she doesn't see you!" Mary muttered, turning back to her sister.

"Who doesn't see me? Portia?" Katherine asked carelessly, enjoying the wicked pleasure of mockery.

"No. Ma." Came the retort.

Katherine's eyes widened and fear flashed across her face as her eyes darted about the room.

"Don't you worry, she's out in the kitchen. But, I'd be a little more careful if I was you!" Mary warned her sister in dire tones. "What if Mrs. Fordyce saw you? Why she'd skin you alive and hang your hide on the mill to cure!" Mary was thoroughly enjoying herself. "And that's only after Pa got through with you!"

Katherine, slightly abashed, was silent.

"Aw, Mary, she was just having a little fun, it's a play party after all." Alice, an only child, put her arm around Katherine protectively. "It *was* pretty funny, wasn't it Elizabeth?"

Elizabeth pretended exasperation and she rolled her eyes upward. Just then Daniel approached. The three girls suddenly became shy and shuffled around behind Elizabeth's skirts.

"Mrs. Scott, may I have this dance?"

She began to tell him "please call me Elizabeth," but a muffled snicker from Katherine and an "oof!" as Mary and Alice elbowed her, caused her to change her mind.

Elizabeth started to explain that she didn't know any of the steps. "I - I can't..."

"I cannot let such a fine dress, let alone a fine lady, just stand and watch!" He offered his arm, then lowered it, suddenly serious. "Forgive me, it's too soon...your husband," he faltered.

Through conversations with the Hudsons, Elizabeth had determined that Dr. Scott had succumbed in the spring of the previous year and that Mrs. Elizabeth Hudson-Scott had been out of mourning for several months, her black widow's weeds left behind in Cincinnati.

"No, there is no need for you to be forgiven, Daniel," Elizabeth said pleasantly. "I am no longer in mourning, as you have already noted by my costume."

Forgotten, Mary, Katherine and Alice faded into the crowd.

And not wanting to embarrass Daniel further by refusing to dance with him, Elizabeth allowed herself be led out among the other dancers. Well, she thought, he's going to discover soon enough that I don't know a Virginia reel from a... from a... Georgia peach!

Immediately sensing Elizabeth's trepidation, Daniel whispered, "Just follow my lead, I won't let you miss a step."

With the warm caress of his breath on her neck, Elizabeth momentarily forgot about dancing.

Portia Fordyce, who up until then, had been gaily dancing with this partner and that, saw Elizabeth and Daniel as they approached. Her eyes hardened and narrowed.

With an exaggerated toss of her curls, Portia fluttered her fan at Daniel. "Oh la! Sir! You have yet to accompany me in a dance!"

Daniel bowed slightly. "Oh, to be sure, Miss Fordyce," he replied before returning his attention to Elizabeth.

The music started up again and after two trips around the floor, Elizabeth felt comfortable enough with the steps to relax and began to enjoy herself. Daniel was a natural dancer and effortlessly guided her through each new set. Despite his gallant promise to not let her miss a step, she tromped on his toes more than once, but it didn't matter, everything moved too fast. Boots clomped and skirts tipped and twirled as the music and laughing faces of friends and neighbors spiraled together in a merry whirl. A happiness and lightness of heart that she hadn't felt in many years began to rise like effervescent bubbles. Her whole body warmed with it and a laugh of sheer delight burst from her lips. Daniel, caught in the contagion of Elizabeth's joy, squeezed her waist even tighter, and looking down into her eyes, laughed, too.

After several vigorous dances, on the pretense of going to see if Aunt Ruth needed any help, Elizabeth escaped to the kitchen to catch her breath. Portia, who had been observing Elizabeth's every move like a cat watching an unsuspecting mouse, immediately pounced on Daniel. She cornered him before he could escape and, with strength she would have died rather than admit to possessing, grabbed him by the arm and dragged him to a pair of chairs set away from the others. Sinking gracefully in a cloud of petticoats, she sat and dabbed daintily at her temples with a lace handkerchief.

"I am *simply* parched with thirst, Captain Mahafy!" She looked up through her lashes at Daniel.

"I'll fetch you some cider, Miss Fordyce." Daniel made his way through the crowd and out to the porch where he filled a mug and quickly returned.

"Oh, la!" That was so, uh, um..." She sought for a word. "Expedient!" Pleased with herself, she sipped at the drink with pursed lips. Then holding the mug away distastefully, she wrinkled"Is something wrong, Miss Fordyce," Mahafy inquired politely.

"Wrong?" she asked innocently, cocking her head so that the curls bounced slightly, a move she felt she had perfected. Then looking at the mug as if she had just discovered that she was holding it, "It's just that these rustic vessels seem to *spoil* the beverage, don't you agree? I suppose once one is used to *crystal...*" She sighed wistfully and looked off into an imaginary distance, her best pose, she thought, of the ones she had practiced in her mirror.

"I wouldn't know, Miss Fordyce, since I tend to be a..." a smile twitched at his lips, "a *rustic*."

"Oh, uh..." Rapidly changing the subject, she asked "Well?" expectantly.

"Well, what, Miss Fordyce?" Daniel asked.

"Well, do I get that dance now?"

****

Aunt Ruth shooed Elizabeth out of the kitchen, but not before she noted Elizabeth's glowing cheeks. Was it just the dancing or did Elizabeth's pink face have anything to do with Daniel Mahafy's attentions, Ruth mused. A musical piece ended and Daniel and Portia danced to a stop right in front of Elizabeth as she returned to the parlor.

"Oh *Daniel!* I *may* call you Daniel, mightn't I, Captain?" She looked up adoringly at Daniel and bared her teeth in a tight little smile that reminded Elizabeth of the frozen countenances on cat cadavers she had been forced to dissect in nursing school. She wouldn't have found it too surprising if Portia had laid back her ears and hissed.

"Captain Mahafy is just *simply, entirely* too formal for such good friends, is it not, *Daniel*?"

Daniel, his face expressionless, introduced Portia to Elizabeth.

Portia slid her eyes at Elizabeth. "I declare, he could *simply* dance all night, Mrs. Scott. I'm surprised a settled, married lady like yourself isn't fatigued by now."

"I am a widow, Miss Fordyce. If you will excuse me please, Aunt Ruth needs me in the kitchen." She turned stiffly, without acknowledging Daniel.

As she left the room, rising over the music, Elizabeth heard Portia trill, in her direction, "Don't forget our excursion on the "Wabash Queene, Daniel."

"Let me tell you a about Portia." Aunt Ruth put her arm around Elizabeth. "Ever since she was a little bitsy thing she's had the finest of everything, no matter what the cost. If someone else had it, she wanted it. And more's the shame, she usually got it. I 'spect most figured it was better to give in than to listen to the fussin'. And I'll tell you something about Daniel. I've known him since he wasn't much more than a child and he is not the type to give in to any amount of fussin'." She turned to slice another pie. "So I wouldn't worry if, I was you."

"Worry about what?" Elizabeth asked, as she busied herself, meticulously straightening a tablecloth.

Aunt Ruth just laughed and gave her niece a gentle push out of the kitchen. Elizabeth was drawn into the middle parlor by shouts, clapping and stamping feet. The musicians struck up a fast tune and to its driving beat, Daniel and two other men, grinning madly at each other, were dancing an Irish jig. A circle of onlookers gathered around and without slowing, Daniel removed his coat and rolled his shirtsleeves. His black hair fell over his eyes and when he tossed his head, droplets of perspiration flew. The dancers' feet moved faster and faster as they circled around each other, never missing a step. The fiddles shrieked and the bodhran rumbled as the tempo increased. Yet they kept up, stomping and tapping out the rhythm with heels and toes of their boots. The crowd cheered and clapped.

Portia Fordyce was right about one thing, Elizabeth admitted to herself. Daniel Mahafy certainly could dance all night.

CHAPTER 18

"I haven't been on a pair of skates for a very long time!" Elizabeth warned. "I don't know how much fun it will be for you to watch this old lady creep around and fall on her, well, you know," she winked at the girls.

Temperatures had remained unseasonably warm until the end of December, when they plunged overnight and ushered winter in with bitter cold. After a week of sub-zero weather, the river and the canal were frozen, but still no snow. The people of Junction congregated at the canal for skating. Those of an industrious bent set to the business of harvesting ice. It would be stored between thick layers of sawdust, preserving it well into the summer.

Elizabeth promised Alice, Mary and Katherine that she would go skating. Aunt Ruth dug around in a trunk and found Caleb's old skates. They were simple in design. Square wrought iron blades curved up at the toe were mounted on a wooden base. The base screwed into the wooden boot heel, which was secured with a leather strap.

"We'll help you!" Katherine volunteered, giggling, although she had just gotten her first pair of skates for Christmas and was still pretty wobbly.

"Katherine, you spent more time *sitting* on the ice yesterday than skating!" Mary scoffed.

"Mary, she was getting much better by the time we went home." Alice said, taking on her usual role, defender of the younger girl.

"All right then, I place myself in your care, Katherine," Elizabeth declared bravely. "We'll sit on the ice together. We'll form the Ice Sitter's Club of America, membership by invitation only!" She placed her hand reverently over her heart, then gave Katherine a squeeze. "You girls had better run along home now, before it gets dark. I'll see you in the morning!" She waved as they hurried off. "Dress warmly!" She called, then shivering; she wrapped her arms around herself, returned to the warmth of the kitchen of the brick house.

****

The year of 1850 was drawing to a close. The White family, after an extended visit, faced with the imminent closure of the canals for the winter, had enjoyed an uneventful return trip to Cleveland. Autumn faded into winter. Rachel and Caleb set up housekeeping in the little cabin down the lane from the brick house. Elizabeth passed many hours with her friend at the snug little log home tucked into a protective bend of the Auglaize River.

Christmas had passed quietly with church services and the exchange of a few simple handmade presents. Rachel's gift to Elizabeth was a promise to paint her portrait. Much of her time was spent with Daniel, Aunt Ruth and Uncle William. Alice, Mary and Katherine, who had come to adore the rather outspoken visitor from Cincinnati, delighted Elizabeth with their frequent visits to the brick house.

****

New Year's Day, 1851, dawned on a sparkling, white world. Overnight the air had warmed a little and soft snow had fallen, blanketing the fields and woods. William Hudson removed his snowy work boots before padding across the room in sturdy knitted socks. He accepted the mug of hot tea Aunt Ruth offered and took it with him to the window, where, with a practiced eye, he surveyed the sky, empty of clouds except for a few mares' tails high in the atmosphere.

"Sun's shinin' now, but it'll snow again before nightfall," he said. Rubbing what he called his "weather elbow," he predicted, "This next one'll mean business."

"Oh dear, Elizabeth promised the girls she would go skating today." Aunt Ruth said, checking the handiwork on the mitten she was darning.

"Plenty of time for that," William took a swallow of tea.

"Winter's just getting a toehold. Reminds me of the one we had to spend apart because I got caught off guard, down at the state capitol."

Ruth sighed. "I certainly do not miss those days when you were representative."

****

Upstairs, Elizabeth swallowed painfully. Her nose dripped and her head ached. She crept downstairs, shaking with a chill.

"I don't think I'm going to be able to go skating." She poured a cup of tea and gingerly took a sip. "I'm not feeling too well. And Daniel was supposed to come along, too."

Aunt Ruth laid the back of her hand against Elizabeth's hot forehead. "My land, child! she exclaimed. "You're burning up! You just get yourself right back into bed. I'll bring you something in a bit."

"The tea is fine for now, Aunt Ruth. Thank you."

Just then footsteps sounded on the porch. Uncle William opened the door and in tumbled four well-bundled bodies. A small terrier bounced up and down on the porch, yapping. Its face appeared sporadically in the small kitchen window. Alice was in the lead with Katherine and Mary, whose silvery curls escaped from their knitted hoods. Following close behind, the smallest bundle of wraps was Charlie O'Dillon, who toted a homemade sled under his arm. The energetic dog, Fritz, was his faithful shadow and only parted from his master with loud protestation.

"I'm afraid I can't go with you today. I'm a little under the weather," Elizabeth croaked.

Disappointment washed over the expectant faces. "Oh, that's too bad." Katherine said. "Well, you can go next time, I guess."

Lisping through the gap caused by his missing top teeth, Charlie bragged: "Ma said my sisters have to let me go 'long, 'cause I'm underfoot." He smiled a broad, toothless grin, proud of his notoriety.

Mary's eyes narrowed and she frowned at her little brother from under her muffler.

Alice sighed. "It was going to be such fun, too! Some of the town boys scraped the snow off the ice. They're going to build a bonfire and roast potatoes in the coals!"

"Would you children like a warm drink before you go?" Aunt Ruth asked.

"Yeth!" piped Charlie.

Katherine whacked him with her mitten, "That's not polite, Charlie," she admonished, happy to be on the other end of an admonishment for a change.

"No thank you, Mrs. Hudson." Alice replied, politely. "Pa says he thinks it's going to snow again and we'd best hurry if we're going to skate."

"Maybe we can bring you a potato, Elizabeth." Katherine offered grandly.

"That's very nice of you, Katherine, but you'd better head straight home after you skate."

The children headed off toward the canal with Charlie bringing up the rear, his sled in tow. Fritz leaped and nipped playfully at his master's mittens.

"Get better soon, Elizabeth!" Mary, walking backward, shouted through her cupped, mittened hands.

Elizabeth waved at them through the window, then turned and spoke to Aunt Ruth. "When Daniel arrives, just tell him I'm ill. I don't want him to see me with watery eyes and a red nose!"

"You go on upstairs and I'll bring you an another quilt," Aunt Ruth said.

Elizabeth trudged wearily back to bed and fell into a feverish sleep. For the first time since her trip into the past, she dreamt of her present-day life. In her dream, she was sitting at the hospital by Mitch's side and the I.V. alarm kept sounding. No matter how she recalibrated the Ivac and adjusted the tubing, it kept beeping and beeping. Her frustration and irritation grew steadily and the insistent noise made her congested head ache even worse, until she woke with a start.

The noise continued even though she had awakened. Then she realized that it was real, the bells from the village churches were clanging like the night of the storm. Pulling on a wrapper, she went downstairs where Aunt Ruth and Uncle William were sitting by the hearth, enjoying the warmth of a crackling fire. “Why are the bells ringing again? It can’t be a flood!” Elizabeth inquired.

“Oh, I reckon some of those town boys think New Year’s Day is a good excuse to kick up their heels and cause a little ruckus.” Uncle William chuckled.

Of course, New Year’s, she thought, having almost forgotten with no hoopla and media hype to remind her. Elizabeth went to the window and pressed her hot face to the frosty glass, looking toward town. She was unable to see much, however, because Uncle William’s prediction had become a reality. Heavy, gun-metal gray clouds hung low over the land. The wind had picked up and gritty white pellets of snow slanted down from the sky. From the icy draft that worked its way through gaps in the door, it was obvious that the temperature was plunging. The clangor from Junction continued, occasionally lost on the wind.

Uncle William joined Elizabeth at the window. “Those boys don’t give up, do they?” he said, a note of unease creeping into his voice. “Maybe there’s a fire somewheres, bound to happen on a day like this. That wind could blow some hot ashes out of a fire-place fast as anything.” He reached for his boots. “Reckon I’ll go make sure nothing’s amiss.”

Aunt Ruth made Elizabeth some hot tea with honey and slippery elm to help relieve her sore throat. The bells ceased to ring at last. The only sound from outside was the wind whistling around the corners of the brick house. Elizabeth’s ears rang with the sudden silence. Then one bell began to toll slowly… clang…clang…clang.

Aunt Ruth gasped, pressed her hands to her heart, lowered her head and murmured a prayer under her breath. She hurried to get her cloak.

"Aunt Ruth! What is it!" Elizabeth asked in alarm. "What's wrong? What does that mean?"

"It means there's been an accident, Elizabeth, and…most likely, a death, she said gravely. "Now you stay here and get back to bed before you come down with the lung fever." Seeing the look of fear on Elizabeth's face, she said, reassuringly: "I'll come right back as soon as I find out what's happened!"

Elizabeth did as she was told. She was worried. Daniel should have been there long before now and Aunt Ruth said he had not stopped at the brick house. Still weak and achy from the fever, she leaned back on her pillow and dozed fitfully. She dreamed again, in little bits and snatches, a patchwork dream. She tossed back and forth and flung off the bedclothes. She was so hot! The dream faded and she didn't know if she had slept minutes or hours. But she did know that something had awakened her. She looked around the room that was almost dark in the short winter dusk.

From a corner of the room came a soft, irregular clattering. Her heart thudding, Elizabeth slowly rose from the bed, peering into the gloom. Someone was in her room, huddled on the floor, teeth chattering. Elizabeth stepped closer. It was a child, a girl… it was Alice Ayres! The girl's eyes were wide with terror. Her red hair was plastered to her head and dripping strands of it straggled over her gray face. Her lips were a dusky blue and she was shivering so violently her breath came in little choking gasps. Her clothing was nearly frozen solid.

"*Alice*!"

With the last of her strength, the youngster held her arms out to Elizabeth and tried to form words. Ripping the quilt from her bed, she flung it around the child, who, at Elizabeth's touch, collapsed into her arms.

CHAPTER 19

Elizabeth scooped up the unconscious child and laid her gently on the bed. She performed a quick nursing assessment and ascertained that Alice was still breathing and her pulse was strong and regular. Removing the girl's icy clothing she began to rub her extremities briskly, trying to bring some warmth back into her cold body. She heard shouting voices and boots pounding up the steps.

Daniel dashed into the room, took one look and shouted over his shoulder. "Caleb!" She's up here! Go fetch Dr. Ayres!"

Rachel rushed to Elizabeth's side. "Oh! Oh, my dear little Alice!"

"She's alive." Elizabeth's emergency training clicked into place. "Go get something warm to drink, tea, cider, anything! Make it weak and put some sugar in it. As soon as she regains consciousness, we need to get some fluids into her."

She resumed chafing Alice's hands and feet. "Daniel, we need to get her downstairs where it's warmer and we need more blankets. Have Rachel warm some by the fire."

Daniel lifted the girl as if she weighed no more than milkweed fluff and cradling her limp body in his arms, carried her downstairs and settled her on the Hudsons' tall tester bed. She was pale, her skin translucent, freckles faded. Unresponsive, her arms and legs were as lifeless as an old rag doll's.

Elizabeth covered her with several quilts while Daniel built up the fire. Dr. and Martha Ayres ran into the room.

"Alice! Alice! My sweet baby!" White-faced, Mrs. Ayres sank to her knees at the bedside, sobbing.

"I think she's just fainted. She's hypothermic. Uh…she's too cold," Elizabeth stammered. She stepped back as Dr. Ayres placed an ear to his daughter's chest, and then, satisfied, stood back. Alice stirred slightly and a little color seeped back into her lips.

"What happened?" Elizabeth asked.

Rachel and Caleb came into the room. Caleb had his arm around his wife, supporting her. Elizabeth noticed that she, too, was pale, her eyes red and swollen. Uncle William and Aunt Ruth returned to the brick house and without removing their coats came to the bedroom.

"Caleb said she was here, thank the Lord!" Aunt Ruth whispered. Uncle William looked in over his wife's shoulder.

A sense of horror began to crawl up out of Elizabeth's gut, spreading until she felt she would scream. Something terrible was at work here.

"What happened? What happened!" Elizabeth demanded, tears of frustration and confusion stinging her eyes.

She was suddenly aware that the room had grown deathly quiet and that everyone was looking sorrowfully at her. Daniel gently put his arm around her shoulder, took her hand with his other hand and led her out of the room. Alice's mother sat on the bed smoothing her daughter's damp hair, tears dripping onto her daughter's face. Dr. Ayres searched through his black bag, silent.

"Elizabeth," Daniel was unable to speak.

Rachel turned and sobbed into Caleb's neck.

"*What*!" Elizabeth begged, frantically searching Aunt Ruth's face.

Ruth, her kind face suddenly old and tired, hung her head as tears streamed down her lined cheeks. Then suddenly, terribly, as realization began to dawn, Elizabeth's stomach heaved and her throat went dry. Daniel tightened his grip on her shoulder.

Uncle William started to speak, hesitated and began again. "Mary…and Katherine," he faltered.

Elizabeth slowly rolled her head back and forth, willing comprehension away, knowing in her heart what he was going to say. "No…Oh, no…God, *NO*!"

****

Although canal specifications called for a minimum depth of four feet and width of twelve feet, the Miami and Erie in some locations it exceeded these dimensions. There was such a place near Junction. When it froze solid in the winter it was favored as the best location for skating.

It was there that Alice and the O'Dillon children headed that first day of 1851. They trudged through the snow, heads down against an icy wind that worked its way through their heavy clothing to numb fingers and toes. The girls forged ahead while Charlie and his sled brought up the rear. Fritz dashed here and there following rabbit tracks, kicking up feathers of snow.

"I sure hope those boys have a great, big bonfire going!" Alice declared, slapping her mittened hands together to warm her tingling fingers.

"Me, too," Mary agreed. "Maybe they'll even have some apples to roast on a stick. I'm hungry!"

"Where is everyone?" Katherine looked around in exasperation. The spot where skaters usually gathered was deserted. Although the snow had been pushed off the ice, no crackling bonfire sent out welcome warmth. There were only cold ashes dusted with the newly falling snowflakes.

"Maybe they're coming back," Katherine said, squinted wistfully through the falling snow toward Junction. "Oh, well, *I'm* not going to stand around all day and let my toes freeze off! Beat ya to the ice, Mary!" she challenged, plopping down on a stump to fasten her skates.

With a whoop of glee, Charlie threw himself on his sled, disappeared over the edge of the canal and reappeared at the base of the embankment as he swooped out into the field. Fritz raced after him, snapping playfully at his feet. Mary, not to be outdone by her younger sister, hurried into her skates and soon joined Katherine on the smooth, gray ice. Alice carefully worked at fastening the leather straps on her skates.

Katherine teetered after Mary. "Hey! Wait up! I'm getting

better, don't you think?"

Mary skated ahead. "C'mon, Alice, hurry!" Picking up speed, she teased her sister, "You'll never catch me, Katherine!"

The girls, warmed by the exercise, shrieked with joy as they raced down the frozen canal.

Pushed by the sharp edge of the wind, fresh snow curled, snake-like, over the ice. It drifted over a crudely painted sign: "*Thin Ice*." The wind had pushed it over almost as soon as it had been placed there.

"I'm coming!" Alice sidestepped onto the frozen surface of the canal. Then, just as she pushed off to catch up with her friends, Katherine and Mary disappeared from sight. With a groan and a crack, the ice opened up and in an instant, the girls were gone.

Alice was too shocked to scream. One minute they were gliding along, waving at her and smiling, then they were gone. There was nothing but a dark pool of open water. Alice ran as fast as she could, never taking her eyes off the deadly, calm, dark circle of water. Encumbered by her skates, she hobbled crazily, frantically shaking first one foot and the other until the skates flew off.

Upon reaching the open place in the ice, she slid to her stomach, while searching for a branch or vine to use as a lifeline. There was nothing. No tree limbs, no vines, no people, no sound. Only the colors of ashes, lead and obsidian: the sky, the ice, and the water.

"*Charlie! Charlie*!" Alice screamed, finally finding her voice. "Go get help!"

Charlie's head popped up over the edge of the embankment and he saw the hole in the ice and Alice lying beside it. Mary and Katherine were nowhere to be seen. He dropped his sled and ran toward Junction, his chubby legs pumping faster than they ever had.

Great gasps of fear tore from her chest as Alice flattened herself as much as possible and inched over the ice. Using her toes, she pushed herself toward the treacherous gap. Frigid water lapped out over the ice and soaked her woolen coat, as, with a squeal, the ice bent downward. Feeling it sag and shift under her, she scrabbled backwards until her boots touched the embankment. There was an earsplitting crack and the terrified girl lunged blindly for the shore. The plate of ice broke and Alice was plunged into the dark water, water so cold it hit her with a shock. Water rushed in her mouth. There was no air! Her heavy clothing weighed her down. She could feel the surge of the steady current tugging, pulling, sucking her under the thick sheet of ice.

Fighting, clawing and kicking, her feet touched bottom and instinctively she pushed up. The drowning girl's head popped out of the water into the freezing air. With numb hands she clutched at a bunch of dead grass that hung over the edge of the canal. Holding fast with hands she could no longer feel, Alice dragged herself up and collapsed onto the towpath, gasping, coughing and choking and free from the stream's lethal grasp.

The current in the middle of the canal, although only three to four miles per hour, was too strong for Mary and Katherine to fight. They were found a quarter of a mile north, under the ice, together in death.

CHAPTER 20

The entire community turned out for Mary and Katherine's funeral at the cemetery just across the road from the Miami and Erie Canal. Maggie O'Dillon, the girls' mother, was supported on the strong arms of friends. She staggered under the weight of sorrow and a pregnancy in an advanced stage. Michael O'Dillon followed behind with Charlie's small hand clamped tightly in his own trembling one. Fritz dodged in and around the feet of the crowd until he found Charlie. The dog sat quivering beside the little boy until the brief graveside service concluded.

Elizabeth shivered in the biting wind. She scanned the crowd, noting the conspicuous absence of the Ayres family. Then, gazing up at the blue sky, she marveled at nature, so cruelly and beautifully unaware of human suffering. The sun shone, but it shed no warmth on the mourners. It glittered off the fresh snowfall that blanketed every branch and twig. Even the simple pine box gleamed - too fresh, too new. There were no flowers to soften the sharp corners. The only darkness, clawed out of the frozen clay, was the opening that yawned in the earth, raw, black and ugly, and the pile of dirt beside it.

A memory flashed and Elizabeth was back in another cemetery, sitting on a folding chair in the dark, suffocating shade of a funeral canopy, with a carpet of artificial turf under her feet. Outside, a relentless July sun blazed down on a crowd of friends, family, and co-workers. Her sweaty hand rested on Mitch's casket and was cooled by the smooth, satiny bronze. The overly sweet perfume of greenhouse roses and carnations mixed with the smells of trampled grass and dusky, moist earth.

****

Later that afternoon Elizabeth paced restlessly through the brick house.

Aunt Ruth looked up from her quilt frame. "Can I get you anything? You are acting like a caged cat." Her forehead wrinkled with worry. "Do you still ail, child? Your fever hasn't returned, has it?"

Rachel carried a pot of tea into the room. "Elizabeth, why don't you come take a hot cup of tea?"

"Sure, that would be nice, Rachel. I'm fine, Aunt Ruth. Really." She turned to the crackling fire and stood there, arms crossed, chewing her bottom lip. Then she turned back, determination in her voice. "I have to go over there. I know I can help! Alice needs me!"

Aunt Ruth looked at her thoughtfully. "Dr. Ayres is a very private, very proud man. I don't know that he would let you see her." She shook her head sorrowfully. "Poor little Alice. She's had such a terrible shock and now the lung fever. I hear she's been getting worse for the past three days now."

Elizabeth's alarm stemmed from the realization that lung fever was pneumonia. Without antibiotics to fight its deadly advance, in 1851 it was most often fatal.

Rachel sank into a chair, her hands in her lap. She spoke in low voice. "I overheard at the funeral today that her fever is so high, sometimes she doesn't even know her own mama." She stood back up. "It won't hurt to try, Elizabeth," she said with quiet determination. "I'll go with you. Pack up the supplies you'll need. I'll get our things."

****

A hastily lettered sign that read: "*Doctor Unavailable Until Further Notice*" hung on Dr. Ayres' office door. Rachel ignored it and rapped on the glass.

A woman in an apron, her head wrapped in a white cloth, opened the door, peered out and prepared to shut it right away. "The doctor ain't available." She puffed with self-importance. "Cain't you read the sign! The little darlin's took turrible sick, ya know!" She attempted to close the door in Rachel and Elizabeth's faces.

"No, wait," Rachel spoke in a firm tone that Elizabeth had never heard her use. "Fetch Mrs. Ayres immediately. Inform her it is of the utmost importance," she said coolly. "Tell her Mrs. Hudson-Scott and Mrs. Caleb Hudson are calling."

The woman, although grumbling, followed her order. She closed the door, leaving the two women standing outside the door in the cold.

Elizabeth looked at Rachel questioningly.

"I know Martha Ayres quite well," Rachel explained. "I think we may have more success appealing to her. Dr. Ayres can be, well, unbending."

Martha Ayres opened the door. Her face was pale and drawn with weariness and worry. "Oh Rachel, Mrs. Scott, how kind of you to come!" She knotted her hands in her apron and looked back toward the stairs leading to the Ayres' living quarters. "I really shouldn't stay away long."

Rachel patted Martha on the arm. "She doesn't even know me, her own mother!" The distraught woman's voice broke and she sobbed into her hands.

"Mrs. Ayres? "Mrs. Ayres, please let me see her." Elizabeth pleaded softly. "Please? I think I can help." She cast about for a plausible explanation. "You see…my husband, Dr. Scott, before he died, did a great deal of work with pulmonary diseases, especially, uh, lung fever." In actuality, Mitch had been a respiratory therapist.

Dr. Ayres was standing in Alice's room, hands clasped behind his back, staring out the window at the bleak winter landscape. The only sound was Alice's labored breathing. He turned at the sound of the three women's footsteps and looked questioningly at his wife.

"Isaac, before you say a word, please listen to me! Elizabeth, Mrs. Hudson-Scott, wants to help us care for Alice. I don't see that it could possibly make things any worse than they are. You're exhausted, you haven't slept in three days." Martha Ayres passed a hand over her eyes wearily. "And neither have I. She says Dr.

Scott had made some advances with such ailments before he…before his…" She hesitated to even speak the word that hovered so ominously over the room.

Dr. Ayres' shoulders slumped in defeat. "I agree with you, Martha." Then turning to Elizabeth, "Mrs. Scott, what plan of treatment do you propose?"

Elizabeth knew she had to tread lightly around this man and his pride and the commonly held prejudice of the day toward women in medical practice. Perspiration beaded on her forehead and upper lip and dampened her dress under her arms. The room was stifling. A fire roared in an iron stove. It must be over 80 degrees in here, she thought to herself. She quickly removed her cape before the doctor could change his mind.

Rachel did the same and ushered Mrs. Ayres out of the room. "Come, Martha, you need to rest a bit, you must keep your strength up for Alice. I'll make you both some tea." To the housekeeper who nosily poked her head in when the door opened, Rachel said, "You may go home now, Mrs. Frankel. Thank you for your services. The Ayres will send for you if you are needed."

"But…but, I hain't been paid yit." The woman pursed her lips, rapidly figuring in her head.

Before the domestic could come up with a sum, Mrs. Ayres reached into a desk drawer, pulled out a handful of coins and pushed them into the woman's hand. "We'll call you if we need you."

The servant's eyes widened glinted greedily as she quickly totted up the amount of money in her hand, then hurried toward the door, fearful Mrs. Ayres would reclaim some of it.

Elizabeth was already rolling up her sleeves when the bedroom door closed. She turned to Alice's father. "Dr. Ayres, what I propose may seem quite radical to you, but as you stated, there really is nothing to lose. To be blunt, if she continues on this course, Alice is going to die. My husband had very good luck with his methods. Please trust me. I love your little girl dearly, she means the world to me and I would do nothing to harm her." In her heart, Elizabeth prayed for divine help.

Elizabeth went to Alice's side and knelt on the floor. She pushed a lank strand of hair from the girl's hot forehead while checking her pulse. It was weak and thready. The last time Elizabeth had seen Alice, at the Hudson house, her face had been pale and cold as alabaster, but now her cheeks were fiery with fever. There was no time to lose. Momentarily she yearned for some modern medical equipment, even simple ones such as a thermometer, a stethoscope and a blood pressure cuff. It was impossible, though, because the first predecessor to the stethoscope would not be invented until later in the year of 1851. A bulky, impractical instrument, it would not be found on the Ohio frontier. Physicians in the United States didn't begin to utilize the stethoscope in practice until the mid-1860s.

Elizabeth set to work. First she removed the layers of quilts from Alice's bed, leaving only a thin flannel to cover her. Then she opened the window a few inches so that cold, sweet air swept into the stuffy room. She asked for a pan of water to simmer on the top of the stove and moisten the air. Then Elizabeth sponged the child with lukewarm water. As the moisture evaporated, the girl's skin erupted in goosebumps and she started to shiver.

Dr. Ayres glared at Elizabeth as if she had let her sanity fly out the window along with the stale air. "I knew your husband, quite well as a matter of fact. He was a skilled physician, quite conservative. I find it hard to believe that he would have sanctioned these outrageous methods." He pointed angrily at her. "Mrs. Scott, you are going to kill my daughter!"

CHAPTER 21

Elizabeth stared through the glass of an upstairs window of Junction's only physician's combination home and infirmary. The first stars pricked through the twilight. The moon was almost full and so bright that it cast shadows. Only that morning Mary and Katherine had been buried in the frozen earth of Junction Cemetery, yet it seemed that years had passed since Maggie O'Dillon dropped the first clod into her daughters' grave. The pain was still sharp and new, however. Tears leaked out from under Elizabeth's closed eyelids as she remembered Katherine's bright, mischievous grin and Mary's earnest expression. She turned back to the bed where Alice lay, each breath sounding harsher than the last.

Elizabeth felt a wave of helplessness. If only she had antibiotics, an I.V., a nebulizer, *anything* to help rid Alice of the infection that took hold when the canal water rushed into her lungs! This despair had washed over Elizabeth and her co-workers many times before during the times when, despite all measures, a young life ebbed away. In addition to the burden of having virtually no modern medical equipment with which to work, Dr. Ayres had been well acquainted with the celebrated Dr. Scott. Even in the throes of Alice's life threatening condition, Elizabeth feared she would be found out as a fraud. If, God forbid, Alice should die, Elizabeth knew she would be held responsible. Stop! Stop! She castigated herself, how can you be so self-centered, thinking only of yourself and your problems, when Alice is slipping away, minute by minute.

She felt anger welling up in her chest. She didn't have the tools she was used to, true, but she still had her wits and determination. In desperation, Elizabeth whipped the sheet off the girl, yanked her fevered body off the pillows and flung her face down over her lap. Starting low and working up, she began a firm rhythmic clapping on Alice's back. It was a treatment used sometimes to help break up the thick mucus in patients' lungs so they were better able to cough it up on their own. It couldn't hurt at this point. Because surely if she did nothing, Alice would be dead by morning.

Dr. Ayres burst into the room. "*Mrs. Scott*!" he roared. He had been persuaded to lie down and rest for a few minutes, but the sound of Elizabeth thumping on his daughter's back must have awakened him. "*What in heaven's name are you doing?*"

"Please, Dr. Ayres, it's a treatment called percussion and vibration. It may help break up the infection. She has to start coughing to clear her lungs! We'll take turns doing this. And we have to get some fluids into her."

****

At three o'clock a.m., Elizabeth, exhausted, had fallen asleep in a chair. The sound of a weak cough woke her. She straightened her head and rubbed the kink out of her neck. There was another cough. Elizabeth sprang out of the chair to Alice's bed. Propped up on four pillows and with her father at her side, the girl's eyelids fluttered open briefly, before closing again. Dr. Ayres looked at Elizabeth, his face suffused with new hope. Martha Ayres and Rachel, sitting at the end of the bed, jumped to their feet.

"Alice! Alice, honey!" Elizabeth coaxed. "Wake up!" In a low voice directed to her father she said, "If we can get her to wake up, perhaps we can get her to drink something! She needs fluids so badly."

Then a realization hit Elizabeth in an illuminating flash. Perhaps there was something Alice needed desperately. Did she feel responsible, somehow for her dear friends' deaths? Maybe in the far recesses of her consciousness she knew the pain and grief that awaited her. Perhaps she didn't want to come back. She had to be persuaded to live, to believe in her own inner strength enough so that she could survive the trauma of Mary and Katherine's drowning. Elizabeth frantically cast about for something that might reach the child and bring her back. She couldn't just sit there and do nothing and let Alice slip silently away.

"*Alice*! Hey, sweetness, it's Elizabeth," she said brightly, staring meaningfully at Dr. Ayres. "Your mama and papa are right here and Rachel, too. We love you, Alice. I…I have a surprise for you! Mama says you can bring Patience in to your room!"

Dr. Ayres hurriedly left the room in search of Alice's beloved cat and returned momentarily with the bewildered little animal held tightly in his arms.

"Alice! Papa went to get Patience and here she is. Wake up now." She took the cat and gently put her on the girl's lap then placed Alice's slack hand on Patience' golden striped fur. The cat, upon sensing Alice's touch, stretched in contentment, licked Alice's hand with her raspy pink tongue and began to purr.

****

Snow continued to fall day after day and soon covered the mound of fresh earth in the little cemetery just as sadness blanketed the village of Junction. Only the relief generated by news of Alice Ayres' recovery tempered the townspeople's grief. Although the child's journey back was slow, during the time she spent nursing her, Elizabeth came to believe that the girl would eventually regain her health. As for how her grief at losing her dearest friends would affect her, only time would tell.

****

Elizabeth spent many long winter hours learning how to quilt under Aunt Ruth's patient tutelage and discovered she was actually beginning to enjoy the disciplined regularity of the needlework. She came to appreciate the taut smoothness of the fabric under her hands and the tiny, even stitches. The names of the different quilts were as picturesque as their patterns: Ohio Star, Sawtooth, Flower Basket, Log Cabin, Bird's Nest, Star Upon Stars, Whig Rose.

"Ouch!" Elizabeth instinctively stuck her bleeding finger in her mouth, but not before a bright drop of blood spotted the calico.

"Don't fuss about that, child!" Ruth reassured Elizabeth. "Every quilter leaves her mark once in a while. After a bit, your fingers will callus and the needle won't poke so. I'll cut a piece of leather and make you a thimble."

Taking advantage of the morning and early afternoon light, the three women, Ruth, Rachel and Elizabeth, joined by neighbors when the weather was open, spent days companionably gathered around the quilt frame.

****

Daniel, who spent the canal off-season working at Fordyce's Mill, often joined the Hudsons for an evening meal. Elizabeth found herself wishing the sun would hurry its descent and bring twilight and Daniel's step on the back porch of the brick house. One night, after a simple supper with Caleb, Rachel and Daniel in attendance, the Hudson family gathered around the hearth. Uncle William brought the last of the apples from the root cellar. Even though they were beginning to soften and wither, they tasted heavenly to Elizabeth, who longed for fresh fruits and vegetables.

Uncle William polished an apple on his sleeve and held it at arm's length. "Reminds me of the times when there weren't any apple trees in the county, back when these parts were called the Northwest Territory and still a swamp thick with hardwoods."

He settled himself comfortably in the high-backed settee he had created with his own hands and tamped tobacco into the bowl of his pipe. "There was this man, a New Englander by birth, a peculiar soul by the name of John Chapman. He was a religious man; held some strange beliefs that folks didn't often cotton to, but we made him welcome. You see, he carried a pack full of apple seedlings and brought 'em to us settlers so we could start our own orchards." William took a thoughtful puff on his pipe.

"Now Caleb was just a little 'un when he come around, just a babe in his mother's arms, so he don't recall it. We offered Chapman shelter here in the house, 'course that was back before…" he glanced at Aunt Ruth, "before the typhoid, so we had a house full o' younguns."

It was way into the fall and a clear night, fixin' to frost, but he refused a bed by the hearth here." Uncle William chuckled. "Said we had too many kids, too much noise and commotion and such! Said he preferred to sleep out under God's roof and that's just what he did! Next mornin' he did take some victuals with us. Well, Ruth was like to have a fit as this feller was barefooted! So I offered him a fine, sturdy pair of my boots I'd just patched up pretty good, but he refused to wear them. He took them though, said he was going to make sure a body less fortunate got them." William paused to take a bite of apple. "I took a look at him and even out in the wilds which is what it was back then, I figgered it would be a long spell before we'd lay eyes on anyone so poor as him. His clothes were in tatters; his trousers tied on with a rope. He only packed enough gear to cook with, his Bible, some religious tracts and those apple trees and seeds. But, he was a proud man and content." William finished off his apple and flipped the core into the fire. "I've seen many a wealthy man since that wasn't near as happy with his lot."

Elizabeth looked down the apple she held in her hand with renewed admiration. It was one of Johnny Appleseed's apples! "Uncle William, what ever happened to him?"

"Don't rightly know, Elizabeth. If he's still alive, I reckon he'd be right old by now."

Daniel spoke up. "About three, four years ago, I had the *Queene* in Fort Wayne. Got to talkin' to some folks and they told me ol' Johnny was buried right there, down by the St. Joe River. Said he'd died a few years before. I don't know if it's true or not."

Oh yes, Elizabeth thought, it's true. It's all true.

CHAPTER 22

Winter loosened its grasp on Ohio in early March of 1851. A balmy wind blew from the southwest and soon all the snow disappeared, save the some of the tallest drifts. In protected areas, green spikes poked through the damp, warming earth. Talk at the saloons and the mill was hopeful that perhaps there would be an early spring. A few of the old timers looked doubtful and warned the gentle weather would not last. They were right.

On a day as gentle as May, the sun shone so warmly that men went about in their shirtsleeves. However, at noon the sky began to darken. The wind switched course to the northeast and the temperature plunged twenty-five degrees in as many minutes. A stinging rain that froze on contact soon encased every surface in a thick coating of ice. Tree limbs groaned and cracked under the weight. As the cold crept back into the house, Elizabeth and Uncle William scrambled to gather a supply of wood from the pile before it was frozen into a solid mass. They slipped and slid around the barnyard, finishing the chores. Exhausted, the family retired early.

Elizabeth, tired out by her exertions outside, fell immediately into a deep sleep, only to be awakened by an odd, orange glow in the room. There was no doubt that there was a fire somewhere and by the way it illuminated the night sky, it was significant. When she heard Uncle William and Aunt Ruth in the kitchen, she hurried downstairs.

Uncle William was already in his coat and boots.

"This time I insist on going! There may be injuries and I could help," Elizabeth said.

Aunt Ruth started to object.

"Ruth, she's a grown woman and she's right, they might need some help."

Elizabeth turned to the protesting woman. "Don't worry. I'll be fine, but right now, I need some warm clothes: pants, heavy shirt, coat and some heavy gloves." She gave her aunt a quick squeeze. “Thanks! You’re the best!”

Appropriately dressed for the weather and more comfortable than she had been in months, Elizabeth set off, following Uncle William. He crunched ahead and she stepped warily into his footprints. As they drew closer to Junction, the fire became more distinct. Flames leaped and licked higher and higher into the night sky.

“There’s only one building in Junction could make a blaze like that!” William Hudson muttered grimly. “Fordyce’s Mill.” Then he added ominously, “Let’s pray to God that it doesn’t take the rest of the town with it!”

Ash and cinders floated down mixing with the snow that had gradually replaced the sleet. Fordyce’s Mill was a column of flame that roared with a wind of its own creation. As William and Elizabeth drew closer, they could see that efforts to save the building were useless. Human shadows ran shouting here and there, silhouetted black against the fire. Daniel staggered past with a bucket of water and didn’t even notice Elizabeth in her men’s garb.

Slowly, one by one, the men became motionless. They leaned on their shovels or stood staring at the out-of-control fire, buckets and pails hanging empty from still hands. The citizens of Junction watched, helpless, as the flames devoured the mill and pushed by the wind, leaned hungrily toward the Fordyce’s fine home next door.

With a screech of timbers and a reverberating rumble, the mill collapsed and a tower of sparks exploded heavenward. Soon after the house followed. It appeared that the fire would consume itself and leave the rest of Junction unscathed.

Over the clamor, Elizabeth heard a woman screaming hysterically. Her shrieks raised the hair on the back of Elizabeth’s neck. Alarmed and fearing serious injury or worse, she ran as quickly as the icy conditions allowed toward the sound. In the ghoulish light of the fire, Elizabeth recognized Mrs. Fordyce. With hands clenched in her hair and clad only in a flannel nightgown, which the wind whipped about her round figure, the woman stood staring at her blazing home. Her mouth was open in horror and emitting the ghastly cries. Portia was trying to calm her mother with little success. Dr. and Mrs. Ayres were striving to wrap the hysterical woman in a quilt, but she flailed her arms about, fighting their efforts to help. Mr. Fordyce approached his wife and spoke sternly to her. The woman sagged against him and quieted immediately. The Ayres were then able to bundle her off to the doctor's office, away from the inferno.

Dr. Ayres tossed another quilt at Elizabeth and shouted an order over his shoulder: "Mrs. Scott! See to Miss Fordyce and bring her to the office!"

Elizabeth gingerly approached Portia Fordyce who stood with her back to the fire. Her arms were folded over a small, ornately tooled leather case that she clasped tightly to her chest.

"Portia?" No response. She must be in shock, Elizabeth thought. "Here, let me cover you with this blanket."

"I can do it myself!" Portia snapped. Her face was smudged with soot, her normally impeccably coifed curls straggled down her back and her slippered feet sloshed in the cold mud. "I don't need any sympathy from you!" She glared at Elizabeth. "I'm just fine. Now, if you'll excuse me, I need to see to Mother!" Attempting to maintain her dignity, which was rather difficult to accomplish in her mud-splattered nightgown and trailing a blanket, she skittered awkwardly across the slippery ground toward Dr. Ayres' office.

Elizabeth checked to see if there had been any injuries among the mill employees and the others who had attempted to control the blaze, then headed toward the Ayres'. She wanted to make sure she was not needed before returning to the brick house. Alice was peering through the glass window of the office and her face lit up when she realized the person that was at the door was not a man, but Elizabeth. She giggled at the sight of her friend in such an unlikely costume.

"Come on, Alice, let's go make some hot tea for everyone."

Elizabeth and Alice sat quietly at the kitchen table waiting for the kettle to come to a boil. Mrs. Fordyce's plaintive voice, mixed with the murmuring of Dr. and Mrs. Ayres, came through the floorboards, but her tone was quieting and starting to lose its agitated quality. Patience sprawled across Elizabeth's lap, eyes blissfully closed, enjoying a good chin scratching. The cat's badly wounded leg had healed well and she held no grudge against Elizabeth for her ministrations. The only sound in the room was the ticking of a clock on a shelf, the cat's purring and the hiss of the kettle. Both Elizabeth and Alice looked up when Portia, with the quilt still over her shoulders, leaned in the doorway.

Elizabeth invited her to join them at the table for a cup of tea.

"I'll remain standing, thank you." She took a sip of the hot brew Elizabeth handed to her.

"How is your mother, Portia?" Elizabeth inquired, truly concerned.

Portia answered blithely. "Oh she's fine. All of my mother's 'conditions' can be treated with smelling salts and a dose of her special elixir." Then a calculating note of hardness entered her voice. "Besides," she said tapping the leather box tucked under her arm, "I rescued the most important thing: Mother's jewels. This unfortunate turn of events *will* set Papa back a bit, I suppose." she sighed.

"I suppose this will be cause for the conclusion of my season in New York before it ever commences! I'll have to pass the entire year in Junction!" She sized up Elizabeth, clad in Caleb's old patched pants and threadbare coat. "But, then you probably wouldn't understand how a truly *genteel* person yearns for culture." She sighed again, deeply. It was such a difficult thing to explain. "Well, you *simply* couldn't understand!"

Alice's eyes grew round as she looked over at Elizabeth, whose only response was to calmly take a sip of tea.

CHAPTER 23

April arrived and with it warmer, but rainy weather. Rachel had invited Elizabeth to sit for the portrait and had been working on it for some time. It was a fine occupation for the rainy spell and Elizabeth packed a small lunch basket and briskly set off for the log cabin. The exercise was a welcome respite from the days of being confined to the brick house by snow and ice and it lifted her spirits. Robins chortled and chirped in the rain and the moist air was permeated with the earthy smell of worms.

Rachel met Elizabeth at the door, and though she usually met her friend with open arms, this morning she seemed weary and subdued. It appeared the long days of winter had exacted a toll on Rachel's well being. Her usually animated face was suffused with an unusual pallor and there were violet shadows under her eyes.

"Hello, Elizabeth. Did you see Caleb on your way? He spied a flock of turkeys down on the bottom ground by the river and decided to get us one." Rachel moved as if her body was weighted with lead.

"No, I didn't see him, but I sincerely hope he bags his bird. And if he does, I intend to shamelessly finagle an invitation to supper."

Rachel's merely responded with a weak smile.

Elizabeth arranged herself in a chair near the cabin's one window. Rachel preferred that location so she could utilize as much light as possible. Even so, the little house was always dark and candles were often needed to augment the sparse light.

After a few strokes with the brush, Rachel's arm went slack in her lap, as if she lacked the strength to lift the brush to the canvas. She sighed.

"Rachel," Elizabeth asked, what is it? "Are you all right?"

"To be perfectly forthright, Elizabeth, I am not feeling quite well today." She wearily wiped the paint from her brush. "I'm so very sorry you made the trip all the way out here today, but I really don't feel up to painting."

"Don't you worry about that! I enjoyed the walk." She turned toward Rachel. "What's wrong?"

Rachel stood up, then grasped the back of the chair as she swayed dizzily. "In fact, I think it best that I lie down and rest for a few minutes." What color had been there drained from her face until it was ashen.

"Rachel! Good grief! Let me help you!" Elizabeth assisted her across the room to the bedstead in the corner. "How long have you been feeling this way? She asked, her nurse's curiosity piqued.

"Oh, I don't know, a couple weeks, I suppose..." Rachel closed her eyes. "Don't tell Caleb or Mother Ruth! I don't want them to get all worried and upset."

Elizabeth lifted a pitcher from the washstand, poured a little water into the basin, dampened a cloth and bathed her friend's clammy face and hands. Rachel drifted off into a light sleep. Elizabeth sat by the window where she waited for Caleb, not wanting to leave Rachel alone.

After a while, Rachel arose, and insisting that she was fine, began preparations for the noon meal. "Don't tell anyone I've been ailing, promise?"

Elizabeth promised, although she wondered how Caleb could possibly avoid seeing how pale and wan his wife was. It was no wonder, she thought, their diet included no citrus, relied mostly on grains, potatoes and game. Her own craving for a fresh salad was growing daily.

Just then Caleb burst through the hand-hewn door, triumphantly holding a large tom turkey by the feet. The bird's head swung limply; its lifeless eyes were open and glazed.

"What do you think of this feller, Rachel?" Caleb asked, hanging his gun on the pegs over the fireplace. He spun the dead fowl this way and that for his wife's inspection.

"Oh, Caleb!" A large drop of crimson dripped from the bird's beak and plopped on the cabin floor. Rachel's look of admiration was replaced by one of dismay as she stared at the blood soaking into the floorboard. Panic quickly replaced that expression as she clapped a hand over her mouth, whirled and dashed for the back door.

Caleb stared at Elizabeth dumfounded, then tossed the offending bird at Elizabeth and ran after his bride. Elizabeth grunted as the weighty fowl landed awkwardly in her arms. Grimacing and holding it as far away as possible from her clothing while still maintaining her balance, she staggered over to the dry sink. With a wrinkled nose, she hefted the lifeless fowl up and onto the sink. As soon as she managed to get one portion of the limp turkey into the sink, another wing or leg would flop and dangle over the side.

She half expected it to take off and start fluttering around the room when she turned away. Elizabeth threatened the feathered mound: "Now you stay put!"

Caleb helped Rachel back in the door. "What's that you say, Belle?"

Elizabeth laughed at herself. "Oh, just giving old Mr. Tom his last rites!"

The fresh air appeared to have revived Rachel somewhat and she went back to preparing Caleb's noon meal. Elizabeth offered to help, but Rachel shooed her out of the way.

Caleb removed the turkey to a big stump in the yard.

Elizabeth was preparing to leave, but took advantage of Caleb's momentary absence. "Look, Rachel! You and I need to talk! When is the next time Caleb is going to be gone?"

Rachel wouldn't meet Elizabeth's eyes and kept stirring the pot hanging over the fire. "Day after tomorrow. Shall we try the portrait again?"

"Yes." Elizabeth smiled at Rachel when she glanced up from her stirring. "Yes, I believe we shall. And have a little talk, too."

Rachel's pale cheeks bloomed with two bright spots of color and she didn't meet Elizabeth's eye.

****

Later that week, Elizabeth was clearing away the breakfast things and preparing for a day of bread baking with Ruth when Caleb stepped into the kitchen, his muddy boots remaining on the porch.

"What is it son, hungry already?" Ruth prepared to cut a square of cornbread.

"Well, some breakfast would be right nice." He shifted around uncomfortably. "Ma…um, could you spare me a minute or two?"

Elizabeth dried her hands on her apron and prepared to leave the room. "I guess I'll go feed the chickens," she said nonchalantly.

"No, Belle, you can stay, you've done some doctoring." Then turning back to his mother: "Ma, I guess I would take a cup o' coffee and a slab of that cornbread and some apple butter would go just fine."

Once settled at the big table, he took a sip from his mug and a bite of cornbread. "It's Rachel, Ma." His face was contorted with worry. "I just hope I haven't done something wrong that's hurt her somehow."

Ruth was instantly alarmed and asked: "What about Rachel?"

"Well, it's a peculiar thing, she's been carryin' on a bit odd lately."

"Odd?"

"Yeah, she's like March, one minute she's just as sunny and gay and the next a'sobbin' her heart out like it was to break!" He hung his head sadly. "And Rachel ain't one to shirk, but, Ma! She just lays about, doesn't cook much any more." He shoveled in another mouthful. "That's one of the reasons I come on up here, to get some decent victuals." He swallowed and said: "Rachel says seems she just can't stand over a frying pan without coming all over woozy."

Ruth thoughtfully sipped her coffee, her earlier concern

eased for the most part.

"Why, even Belle, there, saw how she went all feeble over that tom turkey I shot the other day!"

Elizabeth bent over the dishpan, working with renewed vigor.

Caleb wiped his mouth on a napkin Elizabeth had slipped onto the table while he was eating. "What do you reckon ails her, Ma? Should we get Doc Ayres?"

"Son, I think you had better go home and ask Rachel what *she* thinks the problem might be," Ruth advised, smiling into her coffee cup.

"Well, I believe I will, Ma. Thanks for listening. Soon's I help Pa finish choring I'm going right back out to the cabin."

"Caleb, why don't you just go on ahead, your Pa can get by for one day."

"I can help Uncle William," Elizabeth volunteered.

Ruth's face was beaming as she watched her son depart.

****

That noon, Rachel and Caleb arrived just as the rest of the Hudson family was sitting down to eat. Rachel eagerly dove into a plate of stew that Ruth dished up for her. It was Caleb who picked at the food. His face was a jumble of emotions.

Rachel lavished some butter on a slice of bread. "Caleb, you haven't touched your meal! Are you ill?"

"Wha…" he started. "Uh, no…" He beheld his wife as if he had never seen her before, as if she were a rare and fragile blossom. It was obvious that Rachel had advised him as to the nature of her "odd" behavior.

CHAPTER 24

Rain continued to fall over the Northwest Territory of Ohio. The normally placid Auglaize River and her tributaries flowed over their banks and spread across the low lands of the Great Black Swamp, forming shallow lakes that stretched for miles. Because there was no drainage system, the water stood in the fields for weeks. Some years it stayed wet and marshy through the entire growing season, producing only a large crop of hungry mosquitoes. However, when the water receded, the layer of black silt remaining made for some of the richest farmland around.

Life went on in the busy village of Junction, although all the areas not actually flooded were still extremely muddy. The slippery ooze was everywhere. Planks were laid across streets and roads so that people could pick their way around town. Eventually these walkways were swallowed up by the mud and replaced by other boards that soon met the same fate. Animals and humans alike wore knee-high stockings of sticky Ohio clay. Driving a wagon or carriage through the mire was impossible.

The canals offered the best and most reliable freight and passenger transportation available. People traveled on the passenger packets for "a cent-and-a-half-a-mile and a mile-and-a-half-an-hour." It was slow, but fairly safe and predictable. The canal also provided entertainment as travelers' attire gave rural residents a glimpse of the fashions from "back East."

Daniel's boat hauled mostly timber to the cities. On return, the *Queene* brought coal, oil, and other provisions, such as fabric, tea, coffee and sugar. Also on board were manufactured items from New England: tools, pots, pans and farm implements.

The arrival of the spring of 1851 thrilled Elizabeth like a seasonal change never had before. She breathed deeply of the fresh air, glad to be free of stuffy, smoky interiors. Although women of that day, especially those married, widowed or "spoken for," never went out without some sort of head covering. Elizabeth refused to follow this custom. She liked to feel the sun on her face and enjoy the soft breeze through her hair. On several occasions, when she did not manage to slap her bonnet back on her head in time, she was the object of disapproving scrutiny by a local matron, one of many who already believed that the Hudsons' guest was a little free in her manners.

One evening at dinner, Aunt Ruth presented a plate of dandelion greens dressed with vinegar and other ingredients, with a flourish. Elizabeth hesitated trying them, even though she noticed Uncle William was enjoying his portion with great relish. However, after a long winter without fresh produce, Elizabeth's mouth and gums were sore and a couple of teeth had actually become loose. She knew she needed the vitamins the questionable looking mess offered, so she took a tentative bite and was pleasantly surprised at the fresh, slightly bitter flavor.

Ruth and Elizabeth turned the brick house inside out, scrubbing walls, ceilings and floors. When it was dry enough, they aired bedding out on the tender young grass.

With the shipping season once again in full swing, Daniel was gone most of the time. He still found time to spend with Elizabeth, usually on Sundays. Although he didn't accompany the Hudsons to services when the circuit preacher was in attendance, he managed to be around when it was time to walk home.

Elizabeth knew that she loved him. It wasn't the breathtaking young passion she had experienced with Mitch, but her heart beat faster when he took her hand when they were alone and looked into her eyes. She knew that what she felt was good and honest and stable. There was a solid simplicity and rhythm to her days. Living a hard-working life on the *Wabash Queene* with Daniel was what she wanted. With him by her side, she knew she could love again. She would not be alone.

Elizabeth wanted to belong to this time. With her nursing skills, she would be an asset to these people. She could make a difference! There had even been several letters from her supposed family and friends in Cincinnati, to which she had replied in a rather generic manner. They were received and replied to without incident. Elizabeth knew she could fit into this life. Her needs had always been few, dedicated to work as she was. Though she would willingly leave her past life behind, she feared that the decision wasn't going to be hers to make.

After all, she had just appeared one day. How was she to know she wouldn't disappear without warning and without a trace? At times her life in the 20th century was a mere shadow of remembrance, nothing more than the tattered wisp of a dream. Then there were the moments when bits and pieces of that other life crashed like a rock through the window of her memory. It was then that she knew, yes, she had lived in a time other than this one. When those times came, then she worried. She knew she was fine, but what about Gran and her parents? How long had she actually been gone? Had they reported her missing, searched everywhere, only to find no trace? Then, gradually, no matter how hard she tried to keep her grasp on them, her fears and concerns slipped away, one by one, like droplets of water through her fingers. Once again her existence in the 1851 canal town of Junction became the only life that mattered.

****

By the end of May, Rachel was feeling better and insisted that Elizabeth come so the portrait could be completed. As she was putting the finishing touches on the painting, Rachel stopped for a moment. "Elizabeth?"

"Hmm," she was growing drowsy, sitting in the spring sunshine for so long.

"Did you and Dr. Scott ever…oh, you're going to think my inquisitiveness rude," Rachel hesitated.

Elizabeth leaned forward earnestly. "Rachel, don't you know by now that you can ask me anything?"

"Well, did you ever have…or want children?""

"Oh, well, yes. Yes, we talked about it. We wanted to have a baby, but we…just weren't blessed." She and Mitch *had* planned on children, but fate stepped in before they had the chance.

"Oh, that's a shame." Rachel sighed and dabbed her brush onto the palette. "You are young yet, there's time."

"Yes, I have some time yet."

"Yes, *and* you have Daniel!" Rachel added impishly.

"Hm-m…" was the only reply Elizabeth would give.

Rachel brightened. "Caleb and I have been talking, and if the baby's a girl, we're going to name her *Elizabeth*! If a boy, we'll call him William."

"Rachel! I am truly touched. That is such an honor." Elizabeth chuckled. "I'll be surprised if Caleb doesn't call her *Belle*."

"You know, I've only known you such a short time, Elizabeth, yet in a way, it feels as if I have known you always."

"I know what you mean, Rachel, because I feel the same way about you." Elizabeth searched for the words. "It's almost as if we were connected somehow."

"Ever since that first day when I saw you standing on the towpath, you seemed, well, so different from anyone else." Rachel paused a moment, lost in thought. "It was almost as if you had a glow or a shine about you. Oh, I don't know how to describe it," she said. "You have an *aura*, yes, that's it, an aura."

"Oh Rachel, how you do go on!" Elizabeth said shakily.

"No! It's true! Especially that first day, we were late coming to meet you, remember? When I saw you, it was the most curious thing! You were surrounded by this…this…*halo* of light. At first I thought perhaps it was glare from the sun." Rachel sounded puzzled. "But, it couldn't have been, because the sun was behind us."

Elizabeth wanted so much to share the burden of her truth with her friend. "Rachel?"

"Yes?" Rachel peered absentmindedly from around behind the easel.

"I…I, uh…just about done there?" Elizabeth changed her mind just as she was about to reveal how she had actually arrived in Junction. It was too risky. They would think she was out of her mind.

"Ju-ust about." Rachel started to put her brush to the painting once more, but stopped. "No, there. It's complete as it is." She rose from her chair, a bit awkward because of her enlarging body. Rubbing the small of her back, she asked Elizabeth: "Aren't you anxious to see it?"

"I'm almost afraid to." Elizabeth admitted. "It could be uncomfortable seeing someone else's image of you."

"I think you'll be pleased." Rachel smiled and folded her arms.

Elizabeth stared at the muted colors that blended into a woman's face, *her face.* Not only did the work represent her accurately, it was well done. The color was fluid and full of light, not at all like the stiff, wooden paintings of that time period.

Elizabeth did not possess a beautiful face, yet there was attractiveness there, brought about by the energy that sparkled intensely from the large nut-brown eyes. Although strong about the jaw, it softened into a warm smile. Curly russet hair, reflecting sunlight from the window, was momentarily tamed into the popular ringlet style of the day. The painting revealed Elizabeth's mother's full lips and her father's peaked eyebrows like no modern photograph ever had. The very strong resemblance she bore to her grandfather, with his firm chin and dark eyes that crinkled at the corners startled Elizabeth. Tears pricked her eyes as her heart clenched with a sudden longing for her family.

Rachel was dismayed by Elizabeth's stricken expression. "Doesn't it please you, Elizabeth?"

"Yes, Rachel, more than I could ever begin to tell you."

CHAPTER 25

"Shh! Did you hear that?" Daniel held up his hand, for silence. His team of mules, Dolly and Mae, stopped at his command. Elizabeth and Daniel were walking the towpath, taking the *Wabash Queene* back to Junction. One of his crewmen was at the rudder. Although the sturdy mules supplied the pulling power to move the heavy craft along, it took constant steering to keep it centered in the waterway.

That morning, a warm Saturday early in June, Daniel, Elizabeth and Alice had set off with a laden picnic basket for an excursion on the *Wabash Queen,* whose decks and bright blue shutters and green trim were scrubbed for the occasion. Because Mary and Katherine O'Dillon's death left such a hole in Alice's days, Elizabeth endeavored to spend as much time as possible with the child. Although the girl grieved for her lost friends she did not seem to be permanently impaired by the physical and emotion trauma of her near drowning in the ice-covered Miami and Erie.

"Hey-ey, lo-ock!" Daniel sang out as the boat slowly approached a lock south of the county seat of Charloe.

The lock keeper bustled to the lock and Daniel's crewman leaped nimbly from the boat to assist him in pushing the great red-painted wooden gates closed with the sweeps, or balance beams, as handles, while Daniel, Elizabeth at his side, steered the packet into the open end of the stone walled lock. Dolly and Mae were temporarily unhitched and walked around to the other end of the lock.

"See there, Belle," Daniel said, pointing toward the bottom of the lock gates. "Those little square doors are called wickets. Now watch old Josiah there, see how he's cranking them open?"

Elizabeth leaned over and watched as water began to pour in from the higher level of the canal, and the *Queene* began to rise with the water level. When the lock was full, the canal boat bumped gently against the gates. The wickets were closed and the massive gates on the other end opened.

"Now I understand what that rope is for," she said, referring to the crescent shaped fender, woven of hemp rope, that hung on the front of the *Queene* to protect her wooden hull from scraping against the close confines of the stone lock.

Dolly and Mae were rehitched and the boat continued smoothly on its way. At the little village of Canalport, there was an "exchange bridge" where the towpath changed sides. A stone quarry was located there, along with several other thriving businesses. Elizabeth was surprised for she had never heard of this town, or the two other tiny settlements along the way, called Royal Oak and Timberville. Apparently all had disappeared, along with the nineteenth century, reclaimed by scrub forest long before she was born.

As they pulled into Melrose, Elizabeth looked around in awe. This wasn't the Melrose she knew, with only one gas station, the post office, a small church and a few houses. This was a lively town.

Daniel, mistaking her silence as awe at the bustling little village, said, "Melrose is an up and comin' town, named for Melrose Abbey in Scotland. The lumber, the oak trees, is what's making Melrose. The best clipper ships sailing out of the ports of New England boast a white oak Melrose Mast."

Elizabeth was pensive as she gazed at the immense oak trees. Some of them had to be hundreds of years old. Towering proudly over northwestern Ohio, very few would survive into the next century.

Now, on the way back to Junction, the long summer twilight had almost lapsed into darkness. Elizabeth hoped that they would be hope soon because the mosquitoes were tormenting in their persistence.

"Why are we stopping?" Alice called from the boat, disturbed from her reverie by the slowing of the boat.

Now, as she and Daniel stood listening on the towpath, Elizabeth heard the beep of a nighthawk spiraling downward in the lavender sky on its nightly hunt for the plentiful mosquitoes. A lone bullfrog boomed in the reeds. She heard the first crickets of summer and the impatient stamp of one of the mule's hooves, anxious for oats and rest. Alice was on board the *Queene*, her attention turned intently toward the heavens, in search of the first evening star.

"Shh!" Daniel said for the second time and held up a cautioning hand. "There! Did you hear it that time?"

This time, Elizabeth had heard it - a soft, whimpering moan, much like a wounded animal might make. It was difficult to tell, but the sound seemed to emanate from the woods beside the canal.

"Yes, I did."

"Stay here," he said. "I'm going to see what that is. Sounds like it needs to be put out of its misery." Daniel carefully and as noiselessly as possible worked his way through the undergrowth toward the source of the cry. It was only a moment before Elizabeth heard him call to her in a hoarse whisper.

"Elizabeth, Come here!" To his man at the rudder he spoke normally. "Hey, James, snub 'er up there a minute. There's a hurt critter or something in the woods and Elizabeth would think poorly of me if I didn't allow her the opportunity to offer aid to every lame cricket and cat! Alice, darlin', you just stay put, we'll be back in a minute."

"All right I will. But, be careful, Elizabeth. It might have the hydrophobia or something!" Alice warned. "Papa says he's heard reports of it."

"We'll be very careful, Alice, thank you."

Elizabeth hitched up her skirts and followed Daniel's trail of broken brush into the woods, tugging her dress away as it snagged on thorns and brambles.

"Over here!" Daniel motioned Elizabeth over to what appeared to be leftover canal construction debris, a small pile of boulders and brush.

A slight young woman cowered behind it. Even in the waning light, Elizabeth could see she was clad in mere rags and that her black, curly hair was tangled with twigs and leaves. Crouching down, Elizabeth gently placed her hand on the girl's shoulder, causing her to scrabble away from the touch.

"I won't hurt you! Really, I won't!" Elizabeth was alarmed by the prominence of the bones in the girl's thin body.

Slowly she turned. Elizabeth sat back, dismayed. She was a young black woman, about eighteen or nineteen. Her face was contorted with pain and gleamed with a sheen of perspiration. She cradled her belly with her arms. Elizabeth immediately noted that she was around five or six months pregnant.

Despite the fact that the young woman's bottom lip was caught firmly between her teeth, a sob escaped. "This baby ain't gonna make it." Tears spilled onto her cheeks.

"What's your name? Are you alone?" Elizabeth clasped the girl's hands firmly in her own. "Don't worry, I can help you now."

"My name is Precious. Please, ma'am, please don't tell no one 'bout me!" She panted as another contraction gripped her body. "Don't send me back!"

Elizabeth stared at Daniel, aghast. The girl was terrified. He motioned her aside.

"We cannot take her into town right now. I don't know James, the new boyo, well enough to trust him to keep his mouth shut. You stay with her. I'll…" He paused as he rapidly formulated a plan. "We need the doc. Not because you can't help her, but because, trust me, we *need* Dr. Ayres. He'll know what to do."

Elizabeth was puzzled as to why Daniel felt Dr. Ayres was needed. Didn't he trust her medical talents? "Daniel, I assure you that I have caught a few babies in my time. I can handle this." She glanced over at the huddled girl. "I'm not sure he would get here in time, anyway!"

"No, no, Belle, darlin'! I know you can…it's just that Dr. Ayres has…connections, the kind that this young lady needs. "Believe you me, there are plenty of people around that could use the price that is most likely on her head and wouldn't hesitate to collect on it."

"All right." After a moment of thought she said, "I know. Take the *Queene* back the rest of the way into town, take Alice home and get her father. For right now tell the other two it's a litter of pups abandoned out here. Say that you're going to get Uncle William to bring out the wagon and a crate to put them in and that I'm going to wait here with them, so they don't come to any harm in the meantime."

"Oh you're a clever one, Elizabeth." He kissed her and hurried back to the *Wabash Queene* where Alice was hopping with curiosity.

"What is it? A cat?" She leaned eagerly over the edge of the boat, peering into the increasing gloom of night.

"A litter of tiny pups, me inquisitive lass, and a poor sick mama dog," Daniel replied lightly. When nervous or angry, the Irish brogue tended to creep into his voice.

"Ooh, I want to go see!" The girl started to clamber out of the boat.

"Whoa, there me lassie! "If we don't get you home and out of this damp night air, your ma will chase me around with her fryin' pan!" He gave Dolly a tap and the team started up eagerly.

"What about Elizabeth?" Alice asked.

"Elizabeth will stay with them until I can get Uncle William to come with the cart and a crate to tote them."

"Well, why don't we just take them with us now?" Alice was growing confused.

Daniel forced a chuckle, thinking fast. "I'm just followin' doctor's orders. She says it's best to put them in something to carry them, less jarrin' about, I suppose." He wiped the sweat that was running down the back of his neck with a handkerchief. "Warm night, eh, James?"

CHAPTER 26

The Fugitive Slave Act of 1850 provided legal recourse for slave owners to reclaim their "property" even if the slave managed to escape into a free state or territory. Those who obstructed the arrest of or in any way aided or assisted the runaway faced hefty fines and/or imprisonment. Less scrupulous souls who did not possess a strong moral objection to slavery were often swayed by the large sums of money offered by slave owners for information leading to the recapture of the runaways.

The act increased the need for safe passage out of the country for slaves escaping from the South. At that time, the Ohio canals offered one of the straightest routes into Canada, via two main routes up either the eastern or western side of the state by canal packet to one of the port cities, mainly Toledo and Cleveland, to Lake Erie then by ship across to freedom in Canada.

****

"Precious! Listen to me!" Elizabeth grabbed the girl's hands and forced her to look into her eyes. "You have to remain as quiet as possible. How long have you been having pains?"

"I don't know exactly, since a little after sun-up, I 'spose. I walked until I just couldn't go no further. Someone was to meet me, but I think they got lost. Or I did." She gripped Elizabeth's hands tightly. "They comin' real close together now."

Precious bore the contraction silently. When she was able to speak again, she told Elizabeth how she came to be in the Ohio wilderness. "My man, he in Canada by now. He lef' Tennessee, gone on ahead to Ontario. When he get there and get settled, he send for me. But I got lost at the last stop. Or they miss me, or something, so I started walkin'. I was afraid to stay in one place too long."

As the last vestiges of sunset were gone from the western horizon, mosquitoes swarmed in to torment the two women. A three-quarters moon was rising and offered some illumination where it filtered down through the leaves. By the time Daniel and Dr. Ayres arrived back at the little clearing by taking another route, Precious had been delivered of a stillborn baby boy.

"He gone, ain't he, ma'am?"

"Yes, Precious, he never took a breath." Elizabeth ripped off her petticoat, tenderly wrapped the tiny infant in it and handed him to his mother. "Here, hold him in this patch of moonlight. Look at his tiny little fingers and toes, aren't they perfect? And such a sweet face."

After Elizabeth and Dr. Ayres ascertained that the young woman was not in any medical danger, they left her alone for a few moments to say goodbye to her child. They stood aside discussing the situation.

"We have to get her to Providence," Dr. Ayres declared. "There are people there that will see to it she gets to a ship and to her husband in Toronto."

"Do you think it's safe for her to travel right now? Look at her. She's practically emaciated and has just given birth!" Elizabeth protested in a low voice. "And what about that poor little baby?"

"My dear Mrs. Scott, I warrant that her former owner would have no qualms about her health and well-being should he regain possession. It is far more dangerous for her to stay in any one place long enough to recuperate than risk any complications from the birth." The doctor turned and assessed the young woman who was at that moment stroking the soft curls on her son's head. "She is young and strong, and other than needing a good rest and some decent nourishment, she has all the appearance of a survivor to me." He cleared his throat. "I'll take care of the little fellow. He'll have a decent burial."

Daniel groaned. "That circus is due in town this week. There are handbills plastered everywhere. I heard it was coming in from the west, from Fort Wayne, on the Wabash. That'll bring all sorts of folks into town and a crowd of strangers milling about is not what we need!"

"I believe we have time. Certainly if the arrival of the circus was imminent, we would have heard news of it by now," Dr. Ayres rationalized. "I think Mrs. Ayres and I need to pay an evening call on Mr. and Mrs. Fordyce. The confusion of the circus could be just what we need."

"Mr. and Mrs. Fordyce? Mr. and Mrs. Fordyce?" Elizabeth was completely confused and getting angry. "How can you be concerned about social obligations at a time like this!" Her voice rose in exasperation.

Glancing over at Precious, Dr. Ayres placed his hand on Elizabeth's arm in an attempt to calm her. "Now, Mrs. Scott, I believe I heard the Fordyces are planning an excursion to Providence tomorrow. He knows someone with a mill up there, someone that is quite expedient at shipping cargo into Canada. Daniel, weren't you procured by Mr. Fordyce for this trip? And you know Mrs. Fordyce abhors the sun. She wears veils and gloves, even in the hottest weather. You'll have to see to it that she is kept comfortable in the cabin during the trip." Dr. Ayres raised his eyebrows in Precious' direction.

Elizabeth sized up the young woman. "The height is about right. Add a couple of pillows here and there…"

"Doc! What are you going to tell Alice about those pups we told her we found? She was mighty determined about that."

"I'll tell her the truth, that they died before they had a chance." He paused. "Someday, when she's older, I'll tell her the actual truth, but she's had enough already this year."

Precious lay back, exhausted and heartbroken. As she held her newborn son tightly in her arms she tried to memorize his miniscule features. She wanted to be able to describe his face to his father. She didn't want to forget this child of theirs, born on a race for freedom. She wanted this tiny spark of life, snuffed out before it could flame into being, to account for something.

Elizabeth knelt beside the grieving woman. "Precious, we can't stay here any longer, it's too dangerous. Dr. Ayres can be trusted. He has a plan." She took a deep breath. "But first, we have to bury your son and it can't be done here. Dr. Ayres says he will take care of him. Is that all right with you? That way, he'll be safe."

Precious nodded. "Please, ma'am, could I use them scissors the doctor had in his bag? I want of lock my little baby's hair to keep. And will someone say a few words over him. Before they put him in the ground?"

"Yes, yes, they will. Would you like to say a prayer now?"

"Oh ma'am, I ain't done nothin' but pray over him since you placed him in my arms." She snipped a bit of the fine, black hair from the baby's head. She whispered to him, her lips pressed to the top of his silken head. "Tiny little boy, this way, I'll always have a bit of you with me. I'm your momma and nobody's ever gonna care for you like me. I'll carry you with me in my heart and in my soul, wherever I end up, for the rest of my days. Then someday, we'll walk together again, holdin' hands."

****

Two days later the circus came to Junction. By modern standards, it was a shabby affair: the animals small and mangy, the costumes gaudy and cheap. To the citizens of Junction, however, it was a grand occasion and people from all around the county turned out to watch the procession of several barges come in from the west on the Wabash and Erie Canal. Portia Fordyce was among the crowd of onlookers, decked in all new finery, since the fire had consumed most of what she owned. Her mother, clad in equally elegant attire accompanied her.

A neighbor bumped into Mrs. Fordyce. "Why Hattie! Hello!" She looked slightly puzzled. "I was coming out of the Dry Goods Emporium just yesterday when I saw you boarding the *Wabash Queene*. I heard you were traveling to Providence with Mr. Fordyce, yet, here you are!"

"Yes, here I am, indeed!" Mrs. Fordyce chirped merrily. Then turning away slightly, she took her daughter's arm and pointed to something of interest. "Why look at that, Portia, dear, aerial artists!"

The neighbor's forehead furrowed in confusion, but the tinny band music blaring from the next packet drowned out any more questions.

CHAPTER 27

Elizabeth walked slowly home to the brick house on the first truly hot day of summer. It was humid and her dress clung to her sweaty back. She was tired and her skirts dragged heavily. She had spent that morning helping Rachel with chores at the cabin, weeding the garden, laundry and performing other little jobs that Rachel found increasingly difficult to accomplish. The image of a long, cooling shower flashed fleetingly through her thoughts. Tomorrow would be the first of July. The weather was growing warmer and more humid by the day.

Daniel was supposed to come visit that evening. The *Wabash Queene* was due to be passing through Junction. Elizabeth suspected he was about to propose marriage and was in a quandary as to how she should respond. She wanted to say yes and make a new life for herself right where she was. Lately, however, as each day passed, she had begun to sense a thinning of whatever had been shielding her from her former life. More and more, thoughts and memories from her present day life were flooding into her mind. She felt almost as if she were separating into two parts.

At noon Rachel had broached the subject of Daniel with her usual tact.

"How long will he be out of town?"

"He's supposed to be here this evening. Why?"

"Oh, just curious." Rachel took great care in sipping her tea.

Caleb snorted. "Just out with it, Rachel!" Turning to Elizabeth with a grin, "Do you think you two will decide to tie the knot?"

"Caleb!" Rachel remonstrated.

Elizabeth's face flamed. "Well…I…don't know." She looked back and forth between them helplessly. "I really don't!"

"You better grab him before Portia gets her claws into him!" Caleb teased.

"*Caleb*!" said Rachel

"Well, perhaps she isn't such a threat after all. I heard talk at the mill today that she was right taken with one of those circus fellers."

Both Elizabeth and Rachel brightened with interest. "Really?" They chorused.

"Oh, Caleb, *do* tell!" Elizabeth was happy the subject matter had taken a turn and she was curious about the haughty young socialite.

"Yes, do!" Rachel demanded of her husband.

"That's about all I know. Said he was one of them 'aerial' performers. Flips around on a wire and such." He took a bite of biscuit. "Wears some pretty strange finery if you ask me."

Rachel giggled. "Mrs. Fordyce must be absolutely scandalized!"

****

About a mile from the brick house, the road, not much more than a wagon track, curved and ran parallel as it approached the canal. This was one of the points along the Miami and Erie where the canal actually went over the top of another stream via a trough-like structure of limestone that bridged the creek. It was dark, cool and shady under the aqueduct. Water spilled constantly over the sides and the bright mosses growing there gave the area a tropical air.

Elizabeth stopped to watch a red-tailed hawk soar aloft on a warm current of air, the sun glinting off its wings.

A canal packet that was heading out of Junction approached the viaduct. Elizabeth recognized it as one of the circus entourage. On their way to the next town, she mused. From where she stood, the canal bed gave the appearance of heading uphill, but actually the land dropped away to the creek and the canal remained level. The driver on the towpath was talking to his team of mules, loving and cajoling one minute, cross the next.

As the canal boat drew closer, Elizabeth heard voices. Due

to the distance, the water splashing from the canal into the creek and the muleskinner's one-sided conversation, she couldn't tell what was being said, but it was obviously an argument.

A young woman appeared at the side of the boat, her face hidden in the shadow of her bonnet. Close behind her, an older man placed his hands on her shoulders and attempted to turn her to face him. Angrily, she wrenched away. He tried to embrace her and she shook free again. Before he could touch her a third time, she hiked up her skirts and scrambled up and over the side of the packet. She hesitated only briefly and leapt lightly to the stones of the aqueduct. The man attempted to grab at her as she wobbled on the aqueduct's edge. Frantically, she looked left and right and down at the creek below. With only a split second of delay, the woman jumped.

It seemed that time was frozen as she plunged downward, arms windmilling and skirts ballooning. Elizabeth's hand flew to her mouth in horror as she watched the woman fall. Then with a great splash that sent birds shrieking into the underbrush, she hit the water. The man on the boat shrugged, turned and strolled toward the cabin on the fore deck. With her hands still pressed to her mouth, Elizabeth, looked around and realized that other than the woman's escort, she was the only witness.

The jumper, sputtering and coughing, paddled awkwardly toward the creek bank. Her elaborate gown dragging in the muddy water slowed her efforts considerably. Elizabeth rushed over, found a sturdy stick in the brush and held it out to her. The woman grabbed it and Elizabeth pulled her to shore.

The bedraggled creature lay face down in the mud, her body heaving as she gasped for air. Miraculously, her bonnet had survived the trip and it was still on her head, tilting at a rakish angle. From under the drooping bonnet, strands of moss and dripping blond hair straggled over her face.

Finally getting her breath back a little, the woman, still face down in the slime whispered, "Thank you."

Elizabeth squatted and started wringing out the sopping wet petticoats. "No problem! If we don't get some of the water out of your clothes, you won't even be able to stand up due to the weight!"

The woman on the ground stiffened at the sound of Elizabeth's voice and she slowly rose up on one arm. With the other hand she drew aside the tangle of hair and moss that curtained her face. Her eyes grew wide while Elizabeth's mouth dropped.

They exclaimed simultaneously.

"*Elizabeth*!"

"*Portia!*"

CHAPTER 28

Encumbered by her elaborate ensemble, now dripping with mud, Portia struggled awkwardly to her feet. She angrily pushed her bonnet off her face and, with hands on hips, looked accusingly at Elizabeth.

"What are *you* doing here!" She hissed.

"I just happened to be walking home." Elizabeth tried to keep a straight face, but it was impossible. Delicately picking a long strand of moss off Portia's ruined gown, she smiled and choked back a laugh. "Perhaps I could ask you the same thing."

"*Oh*! Well, I…I…was going to…" The young woman's face reddened. "I don't have to explain anything to *you*!" Her normal haughty expression returned.

"No, no you most certainly do not owe *me* an explanation." Elizabeth smiled sweetly.

"*Mother*!" Portia exclaimed, horrified.

Elizabeth looked up at the aqueduct. In spite of Portia's attitude, it had taken a lot of courage to take that plunge. Elizabeth felt a stirring of respect for the girl.

"That was some leap." Unable to contain her laughter, she snorted. "You should have seen it!"

Portia stamped her foot in the muck. "You've *simply* got to help me, Elizabeth! I can't go back into town like this." She held out her ruined garments, agitated at the thought of traipsing through Junction in her present state. A story could be fabricated, but everyone would know something socially unacceptable had transpired. She would be ruined.

Elizabeth happily envisioned Portia's humiliation.

"Elizabeth…please?"

"Oh, all right." She sighed. "Let me think a minute."

Portia shivered and began wringing out her sodden skirt. "I've lost a slipper!" Her voice quivered. "It was brand new, too!"

Elizabeth thought a moment. "Why don't you say you were on your way out to visit Rachel…and stopped to pick flowers and fell in the canal and…"

"Me, *walk* out to Rachel's?"

"There's a first time for everything. Besides, can *you* think of anything better?" Elizabeth snapped. "May I continue, Miss Fordyce?" She asked with exaggerated courtesy.

"No. I mean, *yes*. I mean, *no,* I *cannot* think of anything better and, *yes*, you may proceed."

"Thank you. So, you had to stop and borrow some dry clothes at the brick house." Elizabeth finished.

"I suppose it will have to do." Portia admitted grudgingly.

"Come on, let's keep on this side of the trees, that way no one will see you." Elizabeth took Portia's arm.

"Elizabeth?" Portia's voice had lost its strident quality.

"Hmm?"

"I suppose you have lost all respect for me…and my social standing in the community?"

"On the contrary, Portia." Elizabeth smiled at her. "I like you more at this moment than I ever have."

"Because you could ruin me with a single word? Everyone would believe the word of the miracle woman–Mrs. Scott–over mine. I have many adversaries, I fear."

"Because you showed a little fortitude back there. Because for a few minutes you let your heart dictate your actions and for once you didn't worry about what people thought of you." Elizabeth paused. "However, I do think it was a wise decision you made there at the last minute."

"Why, I believe that was a compliment." Portia inclined her head graciously. "Thank-you, Mrs. Hudson-Scott."

The brick house was just ahead. Aunt Ruth was out shooing the chickens out of the vegetable garden.

"Well, here's a chance to see if your story," Elizabeth swallowed in an attempt not to laugh aloud, "…floats!"

Portia shot her a hostile look, then rearranged her face into a sweet smile and aimed it in Aunt Ruth's direction.

"Sorry, I couldn't resist." Elizabeth patted Portia's arm and called to Aunt Ruth. "You will never believe what happened!"

****

Portia politely accepted the ride into town offered by William Hudson. Elizabeth stood and watched them bump off to town. Portia's back was stiff with determination as she tried to maintain her dignity in the too large, pinned-up dress she had borrowed.

****

Aunt Ruth produced a letter from her apron pocket and handed it to Elizabeth. "Oh, this came for you."

Elizabeth opened the letter and started reading. Suddenly the hand holding the letter dropped to her side.

"Elizabeth? Is there a problem?" her aunt asked.

"It says I'm needed back at home…in Cincinnati. It says Grandmother is ill. My passage has been arranged on the *Cincinnati Belle*."

CHAPTER 29

"Daniel, I have to go." Elizabeth took his work-hardened hand into her own. "I will come back as soon as I can."

"Elizabeth, I would take you myself and stay there until you were ready to return, but I just today signed a contract with Fordyce. I'll be traveling to Toledo and back for him. In fact this is what I've been waiting for, so that I could ask you…have something to offer," He sighed. "I'm just a canaler. It's all I've known, all I ever wanted to know, until the minute I saw you." He searched for the words. "There you were, in the morning sun, all aglow. I knew you were different than anyone else."

"I - I am different than anyone else, Daniel." How could she explain?

"Could you love me? I know your Dr. Scott was a fine, educated man and that I shouldn't even take it upon myself to insult you with my offer of the canal life. But, I love you, Elizabeth, and I couldn't let you leave Junction without you knowing it. I promise you I'll be a good provider."

"Daniel. Hush." Elizabeth placed her finger to his lips. "I love you. I love you for who you are, not what you can offer me. I think anywhere we could be together would be just fine. Besides, don't you think I'd make a fine boatman's wife? And I'll come back. I'll come back to Junction as soon as I am able."

****

Elizabeth was pulled in two directions at once. She wanted so to stay with Daniel and live a life of simplicity. Yet at the same time, the shroud over her memories and feelings related to her present day life was being drawn aside. She sensed an increasing tug toward the people and the concerns of her life: her family, her career and her unfinished research. What if the letter from Cincinnati in actuality was some kind of message indicating Gran's need for her?

****

"You had best hurry, Elizabeth! The *Belle* is at the wharf!" Aunt Ruth called up the stairs. She was bustling around down in the kitchen packing a hamper of food for Elizabeth to take along.

The past few days had been a whirlwind of travel preparations for Elizabeth's trip to Cincinnati. Her trunk was packed and she was putting a few last minute articles into the carpetbag. She closed it with the nagging feeling that she was forgetting something important.

The adrenaline surge that had kept her going for the past week, since the moment Aunt Ruth had placed the letter summoning her to Cincinnati in her hand, suddenly ebbed and she sagged onto the bed.

She had no way of knowing what to expect in Cincinnati. She knew there was supposed to be family waiting there for her. Who were they, really? She knew she wasn't the Elizabeth Hudson they were expecting. If she had to leave Junction, she wanted to go back to her real family, to go home. She felt as if she were about to step off into total darkness. She was frightened, but events kept moving her closer to the inevitable moment when she stepped onto the packet for Cincinnati. She had no choice but to go forward.

Elizabeth took in the furnishings of her room for what she was beginning to suspect was the last time. She ran her hand over the quilt on the bed and looked at the colorful braided rug on the floor, both lovingly crafted by Aunt Ruth. She tapped the toe of her fine kidskin boot on the smooth wood of the wide floorboards, each hand-hewn by Uncle William, to check one more time and see if she was mired in a dream.

Dashing tears from her cheeks, she grabbed the same carpetbag that had been at her side on the towpath the day she arrived. Clattering down the steps, her heel caught in the hem of her dress and she stumbled on the last step. Uncle William, who was waiting at the foot of the stairs caught her elbow and righted her before she could fall all the way to the floor.

"Whoa there, Belle! We can't be sending you back to Cincinnati in worse condition than you arrived."

"Oh there's no danger of that," Elizabeth replied gaily, trying to cover the quaver in her voice with cheerfulness.

Everyone was waiting at the wharf except Rachel. Even though they had said their good byes earlier that morning, Elizabeth ached to see her dear friend once more. She recalled their conversation that morning.

"I won't be there with you, you know," Rachel said sadly.

"But, you must come say good bye," Elizabeth said, "it won't be that bad. I'm coming back," she said weakly, thinking that Rachel's reticence was because of the emotional nature of their parting.

"Oh, I want to be there," Rachel said. "It's just that, well..." She made a gesture in the general direction of her bulging midsection. "I just cannot, it would be scandalous."

"I just can't believe it, something as normal and natural as pregnancy could force a person to hole up like, like a rat," Elizabeth said, fuming. "There is nothing of which to be ashamed, Rachel."

Rachel's face was pink at Elizabeth's use of the word 'pregnant.' "I know that, Elizabeth, and if it were just me involved, I would go about as I pleased, but I have to think of Mother and Father Hudson, and, of course, Caleb."

Elizabeth was suddenly ashamed. "Of course you do, I just hate the thought of you being cooped up here for days on end, missing everything, and everyone," she said wistfully.

Rachel struggled out of her chair and walked heavily over to Elizabeth and hugged her tightly. "Oh, Elizabeth," I'm going to miss you so. You're so brave and true."

No, Rachel, you are very wrong about me. Elizabeth thought on her way back to the brick house from Caleb and Rachel's. I'm not true and I'm anything but brave. I haven't told anyone the truth, because I'm terrified of what would happen if I did.

It didn't really matter anymore, though, because it is all out of my hands. I can't very well hold up my hands and say: "Whoa, now folks! Guess what! I don't know anyone in Cincinnati, haven't been there since I was a kid and we visited the zoo. It must have been, oh, about 1975. Nope, don't know any Dr. Scott, either. Older sisters Hortense, Dorcas and Rebecca? Never heard of 'em. I've lied about who I am and where I come from since I landed out of nowhere on the towpath a year ago. Okay, now that I've laid that on you, let's get back to life as usual and Daniel, let's set that date! Guess I'll go unpack."

****

Alice was there with her parents. Mrs. Cunningham smiled from beneath a lace parasol. Portia and Mrs. Fordyce were also in attendance. Even Mary and Katherine's family was there, with Charlie and the new baby girl, Katie Marie. Fritz sniffed and nipped at the mule team's hooves, causing them to flick their ears and stamp restlessly.

Elizabeth anxiously scanned the crowd. Daniel was supposed to be back from Toledo in time to say farewell one last time. There was no sign of the familiar *Wabash Queene* or Daniel's shock of unruly black hair.

"Elizabeth!" Alice hurtled through the crowd and hugged her tightly around the waist. With her head buried in Elizabeth's dress she held out a small white handkerchief.

"Here," came her muffled voice.

Elizabeth gently pried the girl from her and held her at arm's length. Tears streamed down Alice's thin freckled face.

"I made it for you," she sniffed. "See what it says: *'Remember me when this you see. Alice Ayres. 1851.'* Oh, Elizabeth, don't go away."

"I'm going to miss you, too, Alice. I wish there was some way I could stay." Elizabeth slipped the bit of linen into the bodice of her dress. She knelt down and wiped the girl's tears. "I will cherish this always. I'll keep it with me always. Now, what are all the tears? I'm coming back as soon as I can!"

She whispered into Alice's ear. "Can you keep a secret until

I get back?" The child nodded eagerly and Elizabeth asked, "Will you do Daniel and I the honor of being in our wedding?"

Alice's face brightened and she stopped crying. "Oh, Elizabeth! *Yes*! Yes, I will!"

Aunt Ruth snuffled into a handkerchief. "Oh, Elizabeth, child! You've brought us such joy…right now, though, I feel as if I've a stone in my heart."

"Aw, now Ma! Quit carryin' on so!" Caleb chided his mother. "She'll be back before you know it! She has to come back and see the baby!"

Ruth sobbed aloud.

"Yes, yes, I'll be back," Elizabeth said absently. She felt as if she, herself, were one of the canal boats that bobbed gently around the dock, only moored by a rope that was unraveling strand by strand. With each good-bye another filament of that rope snapped.

The captain of the *Cincinnati Belle* blew a long mournful note on his horn to alert the passengers it was time to embark. Caleb shouldered Elizabeth's trunk with ease and stowed it aboard the packet. Just then Elizabeth remembered what she had forgotten. Her portrait! She'd left the portrait Rachel had painted.

"*Wait*! Wait! I have to go back! I forgot something!"

Before anyone could stop her, Elizabeth dropped her carpetbag and lunch basket and dashed through the crowd of well wishers and curious onlookers. She hoisted her skirts and ran for the brick house. People turned to each other, speechless with amazement at Elizabeth's bizarre and unladylike behavior. Even those who had become accustomed to her free ways were scandalized.

She raced back to the house by cutting through gardens and past privies. Fritz, Charlie O'Dillon's terrier, yapped at her heels. At the brick house, Elizabeth tore the door open and pounded up the steps to her room. Starting at the top, she yanked at the dresser drawers open, one by one, but they were empty. She sat back onto her heels in dismay. Then she remembered!

Frantically, the woman dropped to her knees and with an

outstretched hand felt under the bed, groping until she felt the roll of parchment. Clambering to her feet, Elizabeth rushed back down the staircase, stumbled, but caught the railing in time to prevent herself from tumbling.

Fritz, who had held a vigil on the porch while she was in the house, immediately resumed his chase as Elizabeth sprinted back toward Junction. Over the yapping, snarling cur at her feet, Elizabeth could hear the moaning of the *Belle's* horn, signaling that that the packet was about to be on its way.

As she puffed around the corner, her sides aching and Fritz snapping at her ankles, she could see Alice jumping up and down and waving in excitement. Caleb was leaning back and roaring with laughter at the commotion his cousin was creating. Uncle William was in the midst of an animated conversation with the packet's Captain while Aunt Ruth stood rooted, her hands anxiously knotted together. Unaware of the spectacle that she made: a widowed woman, skirts in a bunch over one arm, pantalets showing up to her thighs, bonnet bouncing by its ribbon on her back, hair completely undone, Elizabeth waved the rolled portrait triumphantly.

"I found it!"

A cheer went up from the crowd, which had grown. Out of curiosity, townspeople, mill and canal workers, even some muleskinners that had wandered from the nearest saloons, had joined the hubbub. Then from the east came the lowing of a horn as a canal boat, with familiar bright blue shutters and green trim, approached. The *Wabash Queene!*

Elizabeth's heart leaped at the sight of the tall, raven-haired pilot standing easily at the rudder. *Daniel!* A sob caught in her throat and she waved wildly.

Just then, Fritz darted between her feet. She didn't see him under her voluminous layers of petticoats and the dog and Elizabeth's feet entangled. She tripped and fell forward. As she flung out her hands to break her fall, the portrait flew into the air. She thudded flat on the ground, hard, her breath knocked from her body by the impact. Everything went hazy as Elizabeth struggled to get air back into her lungs. The shouting of the crowd faded as a rushing sound filled her ears.

CHAPTER 30

"Lizzy? *Elizabeth!*"

Elizabeth, on her hands and knees in the tall grass, gasped and struggled to her feet.

"*Elizabeth!* Are you all right?"

Slowly and with great effort, for it felt as if her body was stone, Elizabeth turned. Standing there, wearing a perplexed expression, was...*Gran!* Elizabeth's legs promptly refused to support her and she weakly sat down.

"Elizabeth, I swear you're as white as a ghost! What is the matter?" Gran, her face pinched with worry, knelt beside her granddaughter.

"I...I must have tripped...knocked the air out of me for a second. I'll be okay." Elizabeth's rapidly thumping heart was slowing and the vise that clamped her ribcage began to loosen, making it easier to inhale. Perspiration dripped down the sides of her face and neck. Her T-shirt clung damply to her back. The rushing sound in her ears gradually faded away until all she heard was the soft rustle of leaves in the trees and the steady chirp of crickets in the weeds.

She was back! *Home!* The stones of the lock once again lay scattered about by time and the elements.

Crackling came from the underbrush and with a loud yelp, Forsooth launched himself into Elizabeth's arms, knocking her over. He wriggled and whined with joy as he ran circles around her. The ecstatic dog behaved as though she had been gone a very long time. How long had it been, Elizabeth wondered, a moment or a lifetime? Perhaps both.

"Well, somebody is certainly glad you're all right!" Gran smiled at Forsooth's antics.

Suddenly embarrassed, Elizabeth got up, her legs still rubbery. As she and Gran headed back to the brick house, Gran tripped over something in the overgrowth on the canal embankment.

"Oh, that old stone marker. Pap was always dinging up his mower blades on that thing!"

Elizabeth dropped to her knees and tore at the brambles and weeds growing over the object. She had to see it. It was stone, once a pillar, now nearly parallel with the ground, with scarcely legible numbers carved into it: 181. She looked up at Gran and said slowly, "One hundred eighty one miles to Cincinnati."

"Yes, I believe that's an old canal mile marker." Gran gave her a sharp, sideways glance. "Say, are you sure you are all right? Didn't bump your head, did you?"

"I'm just a little dizzy yet. I'm fine, Gran." Elizabeth got up. "It's probably just this heat!"

"Yes, it is mighty warm already this morning!"

Back at the Old Brick, Elizabeth did not argue when Gran suggested she rest on the sofa for a few minutes. "Should I call your mother?"

"For heaven's sake!" Elizabeth said irritably. "I'm a grown woman and a nurse, for crying out loud. I just have a headache, that's all."

Lydia Hudson sat beside her granddaughter, her kind face creased with concern. She took Elizabeth's hands into her own. "My goodness! Your hands are like ice! And in this heat, too. I wonder if you're coming down with something!"

"Gran," Elizabeth said wearily, "I am *fine*. I'm just tired, been working too hard lately."

"Well, goodness, *we* all know that. It's about time *you* discovered that fact."

Elizabeth shivered, even though the thermometer out on the porch hovered at 84 degrees.

"Well, even though you're the nurse, I believe you've caught a chill. I'll go get a blanket."

"That would be nice, Gran," Elizabeth said, "I'm sorry I was so cranky with you." As her grandmother left the room, she was grateful for a chance to sort her thoughts. She looked around, scarcely recognizing the room she had dashed through what she thought was only moments ago.

Lydia promptly returned.

"Here, it's old," she said, holding up a thin, battered quilt, "but most of the blankets are in the laundry. I wanted to hang them out today and get them all washed and aired for winter. I found it the other day while I was sorting through those old cupboards up in your room. I thought you might appreciate some extra space while you're here. I'd forgotten all about it," Gran said as she tucked the coverlet lovingly around Elizabeth. "It was your father's favorite when he was stuck on the couch. He wouldn't admit he liked to be babied, but he never seemed to mind when I tucked him in with this."

Elizabeth ran her hands over the worn quilt, smoothing out the wrinkles and fingering the intricate stitches. Suddenly she stopped and picked up a thin, threadbare corner and examined it closely, staring at the pieced bits of fabric. "Gran?" she said carefully, not lifting her eyes from the quilt. "Grandma? *Where* did you get this quilt?"

"Oh, those big cupboards…"

"No, I mean where did it come from?"

Lydia looked at her granddaughter closely, still concerned about her behavior. "You know, I'm not sure, but I think it was here at the house when I married your grandpa." She placed a pillow behind Elizabeth's head. No doubt about it, as soon as she got the chance she was going to give her daughter-in-law, Elizabeth's mother, a ring. "I think his grandmother made it." She stopped to think. "No, no, come to think of it, this isn't one of hers."

"Oh, I know. This is an interesting story; you'll enjoy this. Maybe you heard it from Pap. I guess with that old quilt stuck away all this time, I just forgot about it."

Elizabeth's mouth was so dry it was hard to swallow, while she waited for Gran to begin.

"Remember last night I told you about one of your great-great-something grandmothers, the artist? You know, the one whose work the historical society is interested in?"

Elizabeth nodded, afraid her grandmother would hear her heart thudding in her chest.

Lydia continued, "Well, she came out here to teach school, it was considered the frontier then, you know, and she ended up marrying a Hudson. I think that would have been Caleb Hudson. Her name was…oh, let me think a minute, I was never that good at this genealogy stuff. I have enough trouble with the here and now, let alone the back then," she chuckled.

Elizabeth bit her lip to keep from blurting out the name: *Rachel.*

"Well, anyway, *she* didn't make the quilt, but Caleb's mother, her mother-in-law did, Supposedly it's made from scraps left over from her wedding dress. You know they didn't waste a thing back then."

Caleb's mother. *Aunt Ruth!* Elizabeth caressed the patches with the familiar tiny rosebuds and forget-me-nots–the delicate hues of pink and blue faded now to pale brown and gray, the shining satin dulled by the years. *Rachel's wedding dress!*

"The sad thing was," Gran was saying, "it was also her burial gown. Caleb's wife never got to see this quilt or her first and only child, because she died in childbirth."

Elizabeth clenched the quilt in her fists as an agony of grief wrenched her heart. *Rachel!* Kind, loving Rachel! How could someone so good and sweet die so young? *Caleb!* His beautiful, dark-haired Rachel wrested away so soon! Was that merry twinkle in his eyes forever extinguished by sadness? A picture of Aunt Ruth came to Elizabeth. Aunt Ruth, her head bowed with sorrow, stitching this final act of love in the dim light of a candle by the hearth – *this hearth.* Tears leaked from under Elizabeth's closed eyes.

"Elizabeth, honey! What's the matter?"

"What's the matter, child? Do you ail?" The warm, caring voice echoed out of the past. Not *Aunt* Ruth - *Grandmother* Ruth! Not *friend* Rachel - *Grandmother* Rachel!

Elizabeth shook her head back and forth on the pillow without opening her eyes. A sob escaped despite her struggle to prevent it from doing so.

"It's just so…so sad!" Holding back the torrent of emotion that coursed painfully through her heart, she asked: "What about the baby?" She had to know, "What happened to the baby?"

A soft, lilting voice chimed. *"Caleb and I have been talking, and if the baby's a girl, we're going to name her…Elizabeth!"*

"Well, the baby lived and was named William after Caleb's father – William James Hudson. Same as your father, only his name was reversed to James William. I remember now! Caleb's wife's name was…"

"Rachel." Elizabeth whispered.

"Why, yes, Rachel. How did you know?"

Elizabeth shook her head slightly. "Lucky guess," she choked.

Gran continued, "Well, the story goes that Rachel's mother-in-law, the one who made the quilt, said: *"Whoever gets William, gets the quilt!"* So, it's been passed down through the family. It ought to go to your father, I suppose, but your mother threatened me not to bring anything else down there, being's that the house is so crammed full now. Your brothers aren't interested either. Would you like it, Elizabeth?"

A sob caught in Elizabeth's throat and she dabbed at her eyes with a crumpled square of coarse fabric. She nodded soundlessly.

It pained Lydia to see her granddaughter so distraught. But, she thought, this is what the girl has needed to do for a very long time. She pried the handkerchief out of Elizabeth's hand and started to mop her tears with it. Then she stopped and took a closer look at the bedraggled piece of cloth.

"Where in the world did you get this old rag? Here," she said, handing Elizabeth a box of tissues from the coffee table.

She spread the scrap of linen on her lap. It was tea-colored and dingy with age. "Look at this, it's embroidered! Let's see…" Gran took it to a window, held it up to the light and adjusted her bifocals. Slowly she made out the letters, reading the hand-stitched letters aloud with difficulty. *'REMEMBER ME WHEN THIS YOU SEE'*...Looks like there's a name here, I'm not sure I can make it out. This appears to be a child's handiwork." She studied the cloth more closely. "It's *A* something...*A...L... ALICE, 'ALICE AYRES'*. And there's a date, but it's very worn here. It's...*'1851.'* My! This is old, almost a hundred and fifty years old!"

She handed the handkerchief back to Elizabeth, who stroked it lovingly as she stared out the window of the old brick house at the hot September morning.

EPILOGUE

The heat wave had finally broken and the windshield wipers on Elizabeth's Jeep clack-clacked as they swished the steady rain from the glass. It was a foggy, misty day and the low gray clouds guaranteed that it would be an all-day rain. She turned from her Grandmother's road out onto Highway 111. Her vacation was over and she was headed back to the city, rested and relieved. While completing her research, she visited the historical society and gazed, once again, at her portrait, displayed with some of Rachel White Hudson's landscapes. The colors on the canvases were no longer fresh and the paint was crazed and crackled with age. The face in the painting was that of a stranger and its hand-lettered placard read "Untitled - c.1851." Although Gran, upon seeing it, had remarked "it must be some member of the family, she's got that strong Hudson jaw, looks just like your grandfather's."

Elizabeth tapped her foot on the brake as the school bus in front of her lumbered to a stop, red lights flashing. Children tumbled out and the big, yellow vehicle started up, only to slow again as it prepared to make the turn onto a county road. The riders all swayed back and forth and bounced in unwitting unison as the bus bumped onto the unpaved road.

Further down the highway, she stopped for road construction. A flagman in a bright orange safety vest motioned for her to open her window.

He tipped his hard hat to the back of his head. "Gonna be a few minutes wait. You in a hurry?"

"No, not really. It would take me longer than a few minutes to go around. I'll wait."

She rolled the window back up and looked at the canal, to her left. At this point it was nothing more than an overgrown ditch. Jagged black tree stumps jutted from the algae coated water.

Suddenly something, a movement, caught her attention. Her head snapped back in disbelief as out of the fog trudged a mule team. Behind them, a heavy towrope dipped in and out of the canal as it slackened and tightened. Attached to line, the long, low form of a canal boat materialized as it emerged out of the mist.

Elizabeth darted a look at the road crew, but they continued their work, oblivious to the apparition on the water beside them. When she turned back, the craft was gliding silently past, the driver tramping beside the steady team, the steersman at his post on the stern cabin, by the rudder.

Frantic, Elizabeth jerked at her seatbelt in order to free herself. She cranked at the window, scrambled around in her seat and thrust her head and shoulders out of the window, straining to see. As the distance widened, the packet grew shadowy. The boat had disappeared. No! There it was! Then, when the vision had almost faded into the rain, the pilot turned and tipped his tall, battered hat to her. Thick, black hair spilled over his forehead and he brushed it back. He smiled, waved and was gone.

A horn blared from the line of traffic behind her. As she slowly got back into her seat, Elizabeth realized the flagman was motioning her on. His sign was turned to "*Proceed with Caution*." She wondered how long he had been standing there, waiting for her to move.

No, no more caution, Elizabeth thought to herself. She shifted gears and the Jeep moved forward, picking up speed.

****

AUTHOR'S NOTE

Although I have taken a storyteller's license in "*A HERITAGE OF THE HEART*," many of the fascinating incidents, people and places in this story are based in truth. My husband's maternal and paternal ancestors inspired some of the characters. They were people who settled along the Auglaize River in the Great Black Swamp of the "Old Northwest Territory," now Paulding County, Ohio. Katherine and Mary Kohart were great aunts who drowned in the canal near Mandale, Ohio on New

Year's Day 1885. It was their brother, my husband's grandfather, little Charles Kohart's, first memory.

The mourning quilt, though fragile, still exists, and is documented in *"QUILTS IN COMMUNITY - OHIO'S TRADITIONS"* by Ricky Clark, George W. Knepper and Ellice Ronsheim, Rutledge Hill Press. The "Old Brick House," built in 1832 still stands by the Auglaize River. Best of all, vestiges of the Miami and Erie Canal still remain in ghostly testimony to a bygone era.

If you enjoyed reading
A HERITAGE OF THE HEART
by Georgia Kohart
and would like to order additional copies,
please complete this form and send it, along with
a check or money order made payable to:

- -

Flying Squirrel Press
P.O. Box 214
Oakwood, OH 45873

NUMBER OF COPIES @ $10.95 each: $ ______
TOTAL AMOUNT: $ ______

POSTAGE & HANDLING: (add $1.50) $ ______

APPLICABLE TAX*: $ ______
(*Ohio residents only - please include 6½% sales tax)

TOTAL PAYABLE: $ ______
(check or money order - please do not send cash)

Name: ______________________________

Address: ______________________________

State/Zip Code: ______________________________